"I suspect this

"Her name is Pea... ...neck tensed, but he forced his tone to remain even. "When you speak to her or refer to her, please do so respectfully."

Everett's eyes narrowed but he didn't retort. Instead, he appeared to take a deep breath—whether to sigh in resignation or calm himself, Hubert couldn't tell.

"All right, I will be respectful. But Father, I can't help but feel you are marrying beneath you. Mrs. Dunnigan likely doesn't make a great deal of money running a boardinghouse for people who can't afford a home of their own." He paused before making his point. "Have you considered that she might be seeking a marriage of comfort and position?"

The tightness in Hubert's neck extended to his jaw muscles. He clenched and unclenched his fingers. Allowing his temper to erupt would not only destroy the fragile relationship between him and Everett, it would also negate any chance to speak of his faith with his son. He certainly didn't want to start out by setting parameters, but he couldn't allow Everett to voice such speculations about Pearl. Distress burned in his chest. Unless Everett changed his attitude, the possibility loomed of having to make a choice between his son and the woman he loved.

**CONNIE STEVENS** lives in north Georgia with her husband of over thirty-five years, John. She and John are active in a variety of capacities in their home church. One cantankerous kitty—misnamed Sweet Pea—allows them to live in her home. Some of Connie's favorite pastimes include reading, sewing, browsing antique shops, collecting teddy bears, and gardening. She also enjoys making quilts to send to the Cancer Treatment Center of America. Visit Connie's Web site and blog at www.conniestevenswrites.com.

Books by Connie Stevens

**HEARTSONG PRESENTS**
HP936—Leave Me Never

# Revealing Fire

*Connie Stevens*

*Heartsong Presents*

To all my sisters:
Those God gave me by birth—Pam and Chris
And those God gave me by grace—
Kim, Eileen, Margie, Susan, Ginger
I thank God for every one of you.

A note from the Author:
*I love to hear from my readers! You may correspond with me by writing:*

**Connie Stevens**
**Author Relations**
**PO Box 721**
**Uhrichsville, OH 44683**

**ISBN 978-1-61626-330-0**

**REVEALING FIRE**

All scripture quotations are taken from the King James Version of the Bible.

All of the characters and events in this book are fictitious. Any resemblance to actual persons, living or dead, or to actual events is purely coincidental.

*Our mission is to publish and distribute inspirational products offering exceptional value and biblical encouragement to the masses.*

PRINTED IN THE U.S.A.

## one

"Oh, for mercy sakes! Stop flittering about like a silly school-girl!" Pearl Dunnigan glanced over her shoulder, thankful there was no one to hear her self-admonishment except Maggie, the cat. Perhaps she should have declined when Hubert Behr asked her to dinner. How preposterous for a woman in her September years to experience flutters over a man's attention.

She propped her hands on her hips and frowned at the two dresses carefully arranged on her bed. Her newest, a dark blue with tiny flowers, was simple, just an everyday housedress. No elaborate trim or fancy buttons adorned the bodice, no special tucks or decorative stitching embellished the garment. The other was her Sunday best. Dove gray with purple ruching around the neck and cuffs and exquisite little purple buttons; the dress was elegant. Every time she donned the dress for church, she pictured fine Eastern socialites sitting down to tea, holding delicate bone china teacups with gracefully gloved hands. The image always made her snort. She'd be as out of place at a fancy tea party as Queen Victoria at a hog calling contest. But every lady should have something special to make her feel dressed up, even for just one day a week, and Pearl loved feeling like a lady. Cooking and cleaning all day for a house full of boarders provided her an income, but at the end of the day all she felt was exhaustion. When Hubert smiled at her, she felt. . .revived.

5

She picked up the gray dress and turned with it in front of her to face the small mirror over her washstand. What would folks think if they saw her on the arm of a gentleman like Hubert in the middle of the week, and in her Sunday best no less? She held the dress against her and smoothed her hand over the precise gray tucks, each one embroidered with purple silk thread. Glancing back at the dark blue still lying on the bed, she knew her mind was already made up.

A knock drew her attention. "Miss Pearl?"

She recognized the voice of Tessa Maxwell, a dear friend who was like a daughter to her. Hastily returning the gray dress to the wardrobe, she called out, "I'm in here."

The young woman with honey brown hair, holding a blond-headed toddler by the hand, poked her head in the door of the bedroom. "We stopped by to see Grandma Pearl while we were in town."

Pearl crossed the room with her arms held out. "Come here, punkin!"

"G'ma!" The little girl pulled away from her mother and ran to Pearl.

Gathering the child to her, Pearl inhaled the child's sweet scent. "How is my sweet little Susan today? My goodness, how fast she's growing."

Susan stretched her hand up over her head. "I dis big."

Tessa gave a sad little smile. "You know I've already had to pack away so many things that she's outgrown." The young mother heaved a deep sigh. "I wish she could stay little."

Pearl nuzzled the little one, her own sigh matching Tessa's. "I don't think I realized all I'd missed by not having young'uns of my own. But I'm grateful that you've let me be a step-grandma." Pearl planted little kisses all over the child's head, and the tot rewarded her with a smile.

"G'ma, cookie?"

"Not before supper," her mother admonished.

Tessa hugged Pearl's shoulders. "I just came from the mercantile. Mr. Behr asked if I could bring in some gingerbread cakes and sugar cookies to the store." She reached out to catch Susan's hand to keep her from investigating Pearl's bureau drawers. "Taking care of a home and a husband, and now this little sweetheart, doesn't leave me much time for baking like I used to do. But Mr. Behr said anytime I can bring baked goods in, he'd be pleased to have them to sell."

At the mention of Hubert Behr, Pearl's heart did a giddy flip and telltale warmth stole into her cheeks. Her mouth took on a mind of its own and stretched into a wobbly beam of pleasure.

Tessa cocked an eyebrow at her. "What's this? A smile through the blush?"

Pearl stroked Susan's yellow curls and shrugged. "Don't suppose I can keep it to myself much longer. I'd like to tell you and Gideon before the whole town knows about it. Hubert and I—that is, Mr. Behr has asked me to join him for dinner tomorrow night."

Tessa's eyebrows arched a notch higher, and Pearl decided to blurt out the rest before her friend's imagination got carried away.

"He—Mr. Behr—asked me two weeks ago if he could. . ."

"If he could what?"

Pearl bent and straightened Susan's pinafore to cover the nervous tremble in her voice. She cleared her throat twice. "He asked permission to—" Her voice cracked. "Oh mercy sakes! He asked permission to call on me."

Tessa's eyes widened along with her smile. "Call? You mean he wants to court you?"

"No, it's nothing like that." Her pulse tapped an erratic rhythm. "He just asked if. . ."

"Mr. Behr is taking you to dinner? That's so exciting." Her friend appeared genuinely happy at the news. "Mr. Behr is such a nice man. Where is he taking you?"

An involuntary smile tweaked the corner of Pearl's mouth. "He said he'd reserved the best table at the hotel dining room."

"Really?" A grin split Tessa's face.

Pearl took a deep breath. "Really. I was just trying to decide what I'll wear when you came in." She crossed to the bed and looked down at the dark blue dress draped across the end of the bed. "I think I'll wear this. It's new and quite serviceable."

Tessa's lips pursed and her eyebrows dipped as she looked over the dress. "Miss Pearl, you're not wearing a housedress for your dinner with Mr. Behr, no matter how nice it might look on you when you're sweeping the front porch." Her young friend opened the wardrobe and fingered through the garments hanging there. "Here. This will be perfect." She extracted the light gray with the purple trim.

"Oh, honey." Pearl lowered her voice like she was telling a secret. "Don't you think people will think I'm being a foolish old lady, getting all gussied up to have dinner with a friend?"

Tessa gave Pearl a quizzical look. "A friend? Is that why Mr. Behr spent every minute with you at the church potluck supper a couple of weeks ago? Is that why he started stammering a little while ago when I told him I was planning on stopping by here, and why you blushed when I mentioned his name? Because he's your friend?"

Pearl took the gray dress from Tessa and laid it on the bed. "Honey girl, I'm fifty-four years old—too old for such nonsense." Susan cackled as though she understood Grandma Pearl's joke.

Tessa plunked her hands on her hips. "Who says you're too old? I don't ever remember hearing there is a certain age at which people are no longer allowed to enjoy each other's company." The two women watched as Susan sat on the braided rug and pulled off her shoes. "Besides, you're a lovely lady and. . ." She leaned forward and finished in a conspiratorial whisper. "And Mr. Behr is a handsome man." She straightened. "And furthermore, I think the occasion calls for a new bonnet, as well. Mrs. Pettigrew is displaying some pretty new things in her shop. She could fashion something for you with some lovely purple flowers on the brim that will go with the trim on this dress."

"Oh, pshaw!" Pearl flapped her hands. "There are plenty of things I can spend hard-earned money on besides a new bonnet." She caught her reflection in the mirror and hesitated. Her hair used to be honey brown. Now there was much more gray than brown. A new bonnet might make her look like a girl again. As quickly as the thought crossed her mind, she dismissed it. Such nonsense. She picked up Susan's shoes. "Come sit on the front porch with me awhile."

The scent of the lilac bushes by the porch beckoned Pearl to spend time with Tessa and little Susan. They settled themselves on the swing, and Pearl reached to tickle Susan's tummy.

"I remember one time." Tessa's teasing smile pulled the corners of her mouth upward. "You told me once that I *needed* to buy myself some new hair ribbons. I think you *need* a new bonnet."

Pearl squirmed "That's not fair. You're using my own words against me." She reached through the railing and plucked a lilac blossom and held it to her nose. The sweet fragrance pulled a soft sigh from her, but the contentment that normally accompanied her brief respites on the porch swing surrounded by the scent of lilacs eluded her. She pushed against the railing with her toe and set the swing into a gentle motion.

"Part of me is afraid of what folks will think and part of me doesn't care what they think. Maybe I'm still trying to figure out what I feel." Out of the corner of her eye she saw Tessa smile.

The young woman laid her free hand on Pearl's arm. "Remember the day we sat at your kitchen table and I told you how confused I was about my feelings for Gideon?"

Pearl chuckled at the memory and halted the swing so Susan could scramble aboard. "Seems to me I recall you asking if anybody ever tried to kiss me."

Tessa giggled. "Yes, I suppose I did. But do you remember what you told me about how to sort out my feelings?"

Pearl shrugged. "I probably told you to take it to the Lord."

"Mm-hmm, that's exactly what you told me." Tessa picked up Pearl's hand and squeezed it. "I can't tell you what to do, but God can."

Pearl sighed. "When did you get to be so wise?"

Tessa's laugh filled the air between them. "Between my mama first and then you, I had two wise teachers."

Perhaps taking her own advice given through the heart of a friend wasn't such a difficult thing to bear. "How about a cup of tea."

"No thanks, we have to get home. Gideon will be looking for his supper soon." The younger woman hugged Pearl and bent to put Susan's shoes back on. "Tell Grandma Pearl she needs a new bonnet."

Susan chortled and shook a chubby finger at Pearl. "G'ma need a new bonnet."

Pearl captured Susan's finger and gave it a kiss. "You come back to see me real soon, punkin." Looking at Tessa and reading her eyes, Pearl added, "And I'll think about the bonnet."

After Pearl waved good-bye from the front porch, she walked back to the kitchen to push the kettle over the hottest part of the stove. New bonnet, indeed. It wasn't enough that she'd be making a spectacle of herself, dressing in her best dress to be seen on the arm of the dapper and distinguished Hubert Behr. Her friend thought she should have a new bonnet to mark the occasion.

She scooped tea leaves into the china teapot and waited for the water to heat. The truth was she wanted that new bonnet. But the sudden desire for the bonnet didn't surprise her as much as the unexpected quiet longing that tugged from deep within her. She'd never loved another man in her whole life but Jacob Dunnigan. She couldn't remember another boy in school who even remotely drew her attention. From the day Jacob kissed her out behind the old willow tree when they were children, she knew he was the one she would one day marry.

She fingered a gray tendril by her ear. After being a widow for twelve years, this desire to be with another man—to be with Hubert—so startled her, she felt like she needed to ask Jacob's advice in the matter.

The kettle began to boil, and she poured steaming water into the teapot and set the tea to steep. She sat and propped her elbows on the kitchen table with her forehead in her hands. No, Jacob couldn't tell her what was right or wrong, but God could. She folded her hands and closed her eyes.

&

"You are a doddering fool!"

Hubert Behr pulled the end of his bow tie loose and began retying it for the fourth time. When his thumbs got in the way again, he sighed and yanked the blue silk cravat from his neck and tossed it on the dry sink.

What was he thinking, asking Pearl Dunnigan if he could call on her? One thing was certain, he was supplying the town gossips with a new topic to occupy their tongues.

He could only imagine what people would say when they saw him parade into the hotel dining room with Pearl on his arm. Sitting together at the church potluck supper was one thing, but asking her to accompany him to a public place for dinner looked like. . .well, it would look like they were courting.

"Courting!" Hubert blew out a stiff breath. He hadn't courted a woman since—"Since Lucinda."

A familiar jolt shuddered through him again. He wasn't sure if it was still the pain of Lucinda's betrayal or the guilt he bore for driving her away that kept him from seeking female companionship all these years. Twenty years to be exact.

Should a man of his age even be thinking about enjoying the company of a lady? He stared at his reflection in the mirror. "Why not?" Was there a law written somewhere that forbade him to take a lady to dinner? The gray in his mustache and muttonchops reminded him he was no longer of the age when one commonly courted a woman.

"But isn't that what I intended when I asked Pearl for permission to call?" Hubert remembered Pearl had blushed to the roots of her hair, but it was her smile and her demure reply that made him feel like a schoolboy. He shook his finger at his reflection looking back at him from the mirror. "She said, 'Yes, Hubert, I believe I'd like that.' That's what she said." He nodded as if reconfirming Pearl's agreement.

"And what will Everett think?" His son's latest letter lay on the table. Hubert crossed the room and picked up the single sheet of paper. Many years had passed since Everett had willingly revealed his emotions to his father. Doing so now indicated the young man cared what Hubert thought. Despite the years and miles that separated them, Hubert had never stopped caring about what Everett thought. He'd loved his son from a distance. Holding the missive in his hands brought a fresh wave of joy. The letter was tangible evidence that the desire of his heart—the restoration of the relationship between him and Everett—was truly coming to pass.

Hubert fingered the corner of the page, reflecting on the

long list of missed opportunities that had escaped during the years his son was reared by his wealthy grandparents. If he could turn back the calendar, he'd do things so much differently. "Lord, You know it is my biggest regret not having been a godly influence in my son's life. If only I'd not let my own faith grow cold during those early years, Everett might have grown up in a Christian home."

Hubert sighed and turned his gaze to Everett's carefully penned words.

*Dear Father. . .* He scanned down the page to the last two paragraphs.

*I, too, am pleased that we are working to put our differences behind us and find a common ground on which to build a friendship. Of course Grandfather was a good man and I admired him, but I am now beginning to understand what I missed over the years by resisting your efforts to take your rightful place as my father.*

*I hope you are now comfortably situated in your new home. Your reasons for wanting to operate a general merchandise store since your retirement are still a mystery to me. I would think after years of moving around conducting investigations for the Pinkerton Agency and apprehending criminals, you would be ready to take your ease. I am trying to imagine you behind the counter of your establishment selling harnesses and work gloves to farmers, and cannot understand your desire to do so. Does your decision have anything to do with the woman named Pearl you mentioned in your last letter? Perhaps you can enlighten me in your next letter.*

*Everett*

The woman named Pearl. Everett's question gnawed at

him. He barely knew Pearl when he decided to purchase the mercantile, so he really couldn't say she was the reason for his decision. But after many months of filling her grocery orders and sitting across the aisle from her in church, listening to her laugh when she played with Gideon and Tessa Maxwell's little daughter, hearing her kind words for friends and neighbors, and finding himself included in that circle, it happened. So gradually he couldn't tell where or when it began. But there it was—the dawn of attraction, like a soft inhalation of fresh air in spring. The realization came upon him so quietly he was mesmerized by its onset until it enveloped him like a glove. The thought quickened his breath.

In hindsight, he suspected her blue eyes were probably the first thing that caught his attention. Watching her eyes when she spoke, he saw tenderhearted compassion and the kind of joy that one can know only through a relationship with God. Her eyes spoke to him even when she didn't say a word.

He ran his finger over the carefully inked words of Everett's letter—*the woman named Pearl*. His pulse accelerated at the thought of telling Everett about the lady who so captured his senses, he couldn't direct his fingers to tie his own cravat. But what should he say? It would take a sheaf of paper to tell Everett about the woman named Pearl.

Hubert pulled his watch from his pocket and his heart caught. Time to go pick up Pearl for their dinner date.

# two

The fireflies danced a captivating waltz in and out of the silhouetted garden, but Pearl shifted her eyes discreetly toward the front window overlooking the sprawling porch.

"They're staring at us."

Beside her on the swing, Hubert chuckled. "How can you tell when a firefly is staring at you?"

She lowered her voice to a whisper. "Not the fireflies. My boarders. They keep looking at us through the curtains."

"Well now, I suppose they've never seen such a handsome couple." Merriment threaded Hubert's voice, and she resisted the urge to poke him.

Pearl clasped her hands in her lap. "Every time I glanced up yesterday in church, Mrs. Pettigrew and Miss Frick were paying more attention to us than they were to the preacher. What do you suppose they're all saying?"

Hubert patted her hand under cover of the gathering twilight. "Does it make you that uncomfortable? Would you prefer that I not come and sit with you on your porch?"

Pearl jerked her head toward him. "No! I would not prefer that." Warmth crept up her neck. She certainly didn't want Hubert to think her forward. "But it does appear that we are the center of attention. It must seem odd for two people of our age to be seen. . ."

The word she started to say faded on her lips. What word should she use to describe their recent activities? Going to dinner at the hotel, taking strolls along the creek at the edge of town, and watching fireflies from the porch swing? Every Sunday for the past three weeks, Hubert had picked her up in his buggy for church, and instead of glancing shyly at each other from across the aisle, they now sat together. The picnic they enjoyed several days ago didn't go unnoticed, and Pearl was certain the town gossips had plenty to discuss over the back fence while they hung up their wash.

Being the talk of the town wasn't one of her ambitions. Lately, however, a feeling she couldn't label or explain away followed her like a shadow. After being so in love with her Jacob since childhood, marrying in their teens, and spending twenty-six years working side by side with him, how could her head possibly be turned by another man?

Hubert quietly cleared his throat. "I believe the word is *courting*."

Pearl's breath caught and her heart stuttered. A firefly pirouetted through the lilac bush, and Pearl followed its path as it laced its way across the yard. Would voicing her agreement with Hubert's assessment be a betrayal of all she and Jacob had together? Jacob was her first love—her only love. Did it blur the lines between right and wrong to welcome Hubert as more than a friend? When her heart looked heavenward, God's comforting nod of approval caressed her spirit.

"Yes," Pearl whispered. "I believe it is." They sat in silence for a few minutes, the gentle swaying of the swing keeping time with her heartbeat.

Hubert reached into his pocket. "I had another letter from Everett. He wants to know who you are."

"Mercy sakes, what are you going to tell him?"

Hubert's thick eyebrows rose slightly. "The truth. That you are a lady whose company I immensely enjoy."

A smile rose up within her chest and found a home on her lips. "Then I suppose you can tell him the feeling is mutual."

The fading light of the evening cast a soft glow over the pleasure on Hubert's face. He stroked his mustache with one finger and answered her smile. The late spring evening suddenly became unseasonably warm.

"Uh, why don't we go inside and read Everett's letter? I made molasses cookies this afternoon. Would you care for some of that tea you like to go with them?"

Hubert's deep, throaty chuckle tickled her ears. "You do know the way to my heart, my dear. Your molasses cookies and Earl Grey tea are my favorites."

Pearl composed herself as they rose and made their way inside. Crossing through the parlor on their way to the kitchen, she noticed two of her boarders peering at her and Hubert over the top of their books. She held back the sigh that gathered in her lungs.

"Miss Frick, Mr. Hogan, would either of you care for some molasses cookies?"

The prune-faced dressmaker pursed her lips and scowled. "No thank you." The woman's gaze flitted over Pearl for a fleeting moment before hiding behind her book again.

Mr. Hogan snorted and flicked a glance at the spinster in the adjacent chair. "I'd like to, Miss Pearl, but I'm full up." He patted his ample belly and gave Hubert a nod, waggling his eyebrows.

"I'll set out a plate on the kitchen table if you change your mind." Pearl stepped into the kitchen and checked the glowing coals in the stove before setting the kettle to heat.

"So, how is Everett?" Although they'd kept company for several weeks, she still knew little of Hubert's life prior to his arrival in Willow Creek two years ago, other than the fact he recently retired from the Pinkerton National Detective Agency. Perhaps his investigator background made him wary of revealing too much of his personal life, but Pearl found herself wishing to know more about this man to whom she felt drawn. "Didn't you tell me he mentioned in his last letter that his grandfather was ill?"

Hubert opened the letter and laid it on the table. "I'm afraid his grandfather passed away."

"Oh Hubert, I'm so sorry." Pearl set a plate of thick molasses cookies on the table. "Was this your father?"

He looked up at her. "No, his mother's father. Everett went to live with his grandparents when he was eight."

Not wishing to appear nosy, Pearl refrained from asking why Hubert's son was raised by his grandparents. If Hubert wanted her to know the details, he'd tell her.

"I imagine Everett is quite proud of you, in light of the number of criminals you've captured."

To her surprise, Hubert shook his head. "No, not really. My son and I haven't had much of a relationship for many years. Up until recently, I'm afraid he wanted little to do with me. He wrote me about his grandfather's illness a few months ago, and we have begun to correspond."

Sympathy filled Pearl's heart at Hubert's pained expression. "I had no idea. But you and he are exchanging letters now?"

Hubert's chin lifted and a small smile tweaked his mustache. "Yes. From what I gather, he has spent some time talking with a minister who came to see Everett's grandfather. It was this minister who encouraged Everett to write to me."

"You must be very grateful."

Hubert studied her, his gray eyes softening. "You have no idea how much this restoration means to me. I think I understand a bit how the father in the book of Luke must have felt when he saw his son coming from afar off. Not that Everett is a prodigal, but the long separation has been very painful."

Pearl poured steaming water into the china pot with Hubert's favorite tea and replaced the lid, letting the tea steep. "He was such a little boy—just eight years old. It must have been confusing for him. You mustn't blame yourself for the estrangement." She replaced the kettle on the stove. "Did his grandparents keep you apart?" She slipped a hand up to cover her mouth. "Oh, I'm sorry. That's none of my business."

Hubert smiled and waved her apology away. "Don't fret yourself. In some ways, yes, Everett's grandmother did have a tendency to stand between us, especially when he was still quite young." He took a bite of a cookie and chewed thoughtfully, as though weighing what to say next. "My wife's mother objected to our marriage, so when Lucinda— that was my wife—left Everett with her parents, her mother believed it was her duty to keep Everett from me. I suppose she felt she was protecting him."

Pearl sputtered. "Protecting him? From you? Why Hubert, you are a wonderful man. You would never harm your son. Why did she think she had to protect Everett from you?" She flapped her hands. "Mercy sakes, there I go again. I'm not usually this nosy. Don't pay any attention to me." She crossed the kitchen to take cups and saucers from the shelf and place them on the table.

She poured the tea into both cups and slipped down into the chair across from Hubert. A troubling thought wouldn't leave her alone, however, and nosiness had nothing to do with her question.

"Hubert, your wife—Lucinda?" She left the rest of her question unspoken, but hanging in the air nonetheless.

"She died several years ago. Her father, Everett's grandfather, wrote me about it. They. . .didn't know where she was. So by the time they learned of her demise, it was a few months after the fact." Hubert hesitated and rubbed one side of his mustache with his finger. "Lucinda left me for another man. After she left Everett with her parents, she didn't tell anybody where she was going. Her parents learned of her death when Everett was thirteen. Her father thought I should know, so he wrote me."

Pearl's heart ached for the little boy whom she'd never

met as well as for Hubert whose wife betrayed him. "I'm so sorry. That must have been painful. I apologize for bringing it up."

Hubert shook his head. "Do not apologize. You have every right to know about my past if you and I are going to be"—the familiar smile found its way back into his eyes—"courting."

"Well, one thing is certain." Like they had a mind of their own, Pearl's hands moved across the table, and her fingers interlaced Hubert's. "You mustn't allow anything to stand in the way of reconciling with your son."

He squeezed her fingers. "I don't intend to."

≥

Hubert crossed another day off the calendar hanging behind the mercantile storeroom door and frowned. June 18. If his order didn't arrive within a few days, he'd have to do some quick thinking. Almost two months ago he'd ordered a silver music box from a distributor in Philadelphia. Mermod Freres created some of the finest musical boxes made, and Hubert chose one especially for Pearl's birthday. But he had another reason for wanting her birthday to be special—a reason that tied his stomach in a knot.

He'd imagined the delight in Pearl's eyes, but his plans to make the day memorable might turn out less than perfect if the music box didn't arrive. He rubbed his hand over his whiskered chin. For all he knew, the music box was sitting in some freight office in Dubuque. If only Willow Creek had a freight company, he'd likely already have his special surprise for Pearl in hand.

"Nothing to be gained by fretting."

Hubert set to work unpacking crates and restocking shelves. Despite exchanging pleasantries with townsfolk who came in to make purchases, Hubert's mind wasn't far from the twinkling blue eyes that held his heart captive.

But a disturbing cloud hung over him. It wasn't the delayed delivery of the music box. This was deeper, more troubling.

As a Pinkerton detective, he'd learned years ago to leash his emotions. Masking the turbulence occurring on the inside made him a successful detective for the agency. Pearl considered him some kind of hero for apprehending the unscrupulous man who'd defrauded many of the folks in Willow Creek two years ago, but doubt gnawed at him and regrets swirled over his head like vultures. Forgiveness was something for which he hungered.

The mercantile was quiet for the moment. He stepped into the storeroom. "Lord, I never want to make those same mistakes again. I didn't listen to You when I should have, and remorse has been my constant companion all these years. Can You use me now if I wasn't usable then?"

Everett's letters, however welcomed, also reminded him of his shortcomings. He'd been able to keep the sins of his past buried for years to those around him, but there was one person who knew—Everett. The joy he savored over the reconciliation with his son brought with it a hint of bitterness.

The bell on the front door jingled, announcing the arrival of a customer. Hubert blinked the moisture from his eyes and reentered the front of the store. Pearl stood there smiling, a market basket over her arm.

"Good morning, Hubert." Every smile she bestowed on him was a gift.

His heart quickened and a tremble tiptoed through him. "Good morning. I was just thinking about you earlier, and I had an idea."

Pearl set her basket on the counter and adjusted her bonnet. "What kind of idea?"

He cupped his chin between his thumb and index finger. "A little bird told me that Sunday is your birthday."

Pearl's eyes narrowed. "Was the bird's name Tessa?"

A smile tipped the corners of Hubert's mouth. "Possibly." He clasped his hands together and laid them on the counter. "I would like very much to take you on a picnic to celebrate your birthday."

A small frown dented her brow. "But I have to make dinner for my boarders."

Hubert nodded and pressed his fingertips together. "Do you think they would mind fending for themselves just this once? Since it's your birthday?"

Pearl cocked her head and placed a finger on her chin. "I suppose I could ask Mrs. Russell to manage dinner. She keeps telling me what a good cook she is." She bit her lip. "I didn't mean that the way it sounded."

Hubert chuckled and took her hand, lifting it to his lips to deliver a kiss to her fingertips. "Then it's settled. If Mrs. Russell is agreeable, I will look forward to our picnic on Sunday." If she only knew how much. "Now what can I get for you today?"

She handed him her shopping list and browsed around the store. While he measured coffee beans, cornmeal, and sugar, he watched her finger the edge of a bolt of calico. When he was in the same room with her, he could barely take his eyes off her. When they were apart, loneliness ached in his heart.

He deposited the last item in Pearl's basket. "Was there anything else?"

"That's all for today." She paid for her purchases and gave him a modest smile. "Thank you, sir."

Hubert took the basket and walked her to the door. "May I pick you up for church at the usual time this Sunday?"

"Of course. I'm looking forward to our picnic."

"As am I." He handed her the basket. The memory of her smile would have to last him until Sunday. He prayed the music box would arrive in time.

Hubert couldn't remember being this nervous facing the most notorious criminal. If the church service had gone on another five minutes, he might have jumped out of his skin. As it was, he could barely remember what the pastor preached about, spending the time instead praying God would calm his pounding pulse. When the final hymn was sung, Hubert escorted Pearl to the front door of the church where they shook hands and exchanged pleasantries with the pastor. After assisting her into the buggy, he drove to a quiet grove of birches near the edge of town beside the tumbling creek. Several huge willows hung over the water like a curtain. He pulled a quilt and a picnic basket from beneath the buggy seat and extended a hand to help Pearl disembark. When she was safely on the ground, he didn't let go of her hand but gave it a gentle squeeze as they selected a shady spot. Did she feel the tremor in his hand?

They spread out their picnic near the willow trees where they could watch the creek play over the rocks. Despite the delectable fried chicken and potato salad prepared by Tessa, Hubert could barely swallow a bite, wondering if Pearl could hear his galloping heart. When they finished their meal, he reached into the basket and extracted a small beribboned box wrapped in tissue paper and set it on the blanket in front of Pearl.

"For you, my dear."

Her mouth formed an *O*. "Mercy sakes, Hubert, you're going to spoil me."

"I hope so."

She opened the box and gave a soft gasp. She lifted the silver music box and found the tiny key on the side. Two gentle twists of the key and a Strauss waltz wafted on the breeze.

"Hubert, this is lovely." Moisture glistened in her eyes.

Hubert's breath shortened as his pulse raced. The time had come for him to reveal his heart to her. He took her hands in his. "I must tell you, dear Pearl, that this isn't really a birthday gift."

Pearl blinked and looked askance. "It's not?"

Hubert shook his head and started to rise but halted midway and went to one knee, Pearl's hand in his. Her eyes widened and her lips parted. His heart pounded like a blacksmith's hammer on an anvil. Sweat dampened his palms. "I am hoping it will serve as an engagement gift. That is, if you will have me. I love you, Pearl Dunnigan, and I never wish to be parted from you. Will you consent to be my wife?"

# three

Pearl studied the floral print of the wallpaper in the boardinghouse dining room as she listened to Hubert's pen scritch-scritching across the stationery. Apprehension knotted her stomach. When she accepted Hubert's proposal one week ago, he suggested they write his son together, letting Everett know of their engagement.

Hubert reached across the dining table and patted her hand. "What date should I tell him we've set for the wedding? I'm not sure if he would be able to come, but if we give him enough notice, perhaps. . ."

Though he left the sentence unfinished, Pearl read his thoughts. "How long has it been since you've seen Everett?"

Hubert leaned back in his chair, the pen paused over the page. "Just over four years. I went to see him when I received word of his grandmother's death. The reception he gave me was rather cold."

"But that was before the two of you began corresponding. The letters you've shared with me sound like Everett is anxious for a restored relationship." Pearl hoped the optimism in her statement encouraged Hubert's heart, even while misgivings prodded her own. Given the fact Everett was an adult, would he think she was trying to take his mother's place? At the very least, he might consider her marriage to his father an intrusion into their fragile bond. She took a slow, deep breath.

"Hubert, you know I never had children of my own. I'd always hoped to give Jacob a son, but the Lord didn't see fit to allow it. Tessa Maxwell is like a daughter to me, and I'm delighted to play the role of step-grandma to little Susan."

She paused and bit her lip. "But I must admit the idea of suddenly becoming a stepmother makes me a bit nervous, even if Everett is a grown man."

Hubert's thick eyebrows rose as he looked at her with surprise. "Now why should you be nervous?"

She tilted her head to one side and huffed out a soft breath. "He's never met me. His father is marrying a complete stranger. What if he doesn't like me?"

A mirth-filled chuckle bubbled from him. "That, my dear, is quite impossible." He dipped the nib into the inkwell. "So, today is June twenty-ninth. If you want a June wedding, we'll have to get married tomorrow or wait a whole year."

A June wedding. Dreaming of being a June bride was for young girls, not matronly women, but even as the romantic notion filled her mind, she giggled. "At our ages, waiting a whole year probably wouldn't be a good idea." She smiled and allowed the picture to form in her mind. Wouldn't it be lovely for her and Hubert to stand amid the apple blossoms in her backyard?

Her backyard. "Oh." She placed her fingers over her mouth. "Hubert, we haven't discussed where we'll live after the wedding."

A twinge of regret flicked across his features. "I'm sorry, Pearl. I've been making decisions for so long, taking nobody but myself into consideration. I suppose I need to work on changing my habits." A repentant grin tilted his mouth. "When I had my house built last year, I didn't exactly design it with the idea I'd one day bring a wife home, but it surely could use a woman's touch. When I first imagined asking you to marry me, I just assumed you'd move to my home." He laid the pen aside. "It was boorish of me to be so presumptuous. Did you have other thoughts?"

Pearl looked about the boardinghouse dining room. "It didn't occur to me until now, but I suppose I'll have to sell the boardinghouse."

Hubert's gaze turned apologetic. "Would that distress you?"

More than a decade of memories filled the walls of the old house. Some happy, others not so. Several of the boarders who'd resided there over the years had become like family to her, and the house itself symbolized God's provision, the means He gave her to support herself after Jacob's death. Running the place was hard work, especially after Tessa married and moved out. Even though Tessa had only resided at the boardinghouse for a year, Pearl enjoyed her help while she was there and missed it when she left. Every passing year new repairs had to be performed. Hubert's proposal meant a new chapter in her life. She contemplated the answer to Hubert's question. Would she regret selling the place?

"No, not really." Her spirit agreed with her response. "Sometimes it's hard to say good-bye to one's yesterdays, but I believe God is telling me it's time to build some tomorrows with you." She gave him a wobbly smile. "I'd love to be married as soon as possible, but what if it takes awhile to sell the boardinghouse?"

Hubert waved his fingers. "There's no need to fret over that." He stroked his chin. "What would you think about asking one of your lady boarders to take over the operation in exchange for free rent and a small stipend?"

She pondered the possibility and nodded. "Yes, I suppose that's a possibility. Miss Pendergrass, the schoolteacher, has moved out now that school has closed for the summer, so there are currently only four boarders. Mrs. Russell might be interested in such an arrangement. I'll talk to her this evening."

He returned her smile and picked up the pen. Speaking the words aloud as he wrote them, he continued the letter to Everett. "We are hoping to be married soon. I hope you can come, as I am anxious to introduce you to my bride. With warmest regards, Father."

Hubert blew on the page to hasten the drying of the ink. "Would you like to add a personal note?" He held the pen out to her.

Pearl's breath caught. What should she say to the young man she'd never met, but whose father had stolen her heart? She hesitated, then took the pen from Hubert and dipped it into the ink pot.

*Dear Everett,*
*  I am so grateful God has brought your father into my life. We both pray you can come to Willow Creek for the wedding. I look forward to meeting you.*

*Pearl Dunnigan*

Hubert folded the letter and tucked it into the envelope. "You know, there were many days—many years, actually—that I thought I'd never be this happy again." A tiny muscle twitched downward on the corner of his mouth, and he rubbed his finger over his mustache. Pearl had grown accustomed to the gesture. It seemed to be an unconscious habit Hubert did whenever he contemplated a matter. She waited in silence for him to continue.

"The weeks and months after my wife left were terribly painful." He hesitated as though carefully weighing his words. "As the months turned into years, I thought it would become easier to deal with the loneliness. By the time I got word of Lucinda's death, Everett had already built up a rather formidable dislike of me." A troubled, faraway look crept into his eyes and the tone of his voice changed, like he was speaking to some unseen person. "I wondered if perhaps God had decided I wasn't worthy of happiness."

"Hubert, how can you say such a thing?" Pearl's heart pinched as she listened to Hubert's words. "You are as well-acquainted with God's love as I am."

As if someone snapped their fingers, Hubert abruptly returned his attention to her. He picked up her hand and kissed her fingertips. "Indeed, I am. What do you say we go for a walk to work off your delicious Sunday dinner?"

"Just let me get my shawl." She rose and hurried to her bedroom, anticipating the late afternoon stroll in the early summer air. But Hubert's pensive speculation echoed in her heart. How could he think God didn't desire his happiness?

&

Pearl gave the worktable one last wipe and hung the damp rag on the back of the pantry door. Hubert's troubling words dogged her thoughts all evening. When she'd attempted to bring up the topic again, he'd brushed it off as inconsequential, and she could only wonder at the past memories that must have prompted such a statement. He'd bidden her good night earlier than usual, claiming a headache.

"Lord, maybe I do understand a little of how Hubert must have felt." She slipped into her bedroom and closed the door. Lowering herself to the chair at her dressing table, she began unpinning her gray hair. "When Jacob went home to be with You, I never thought I'd love again." But she suspected it was something more than loneliness that induced Hubert's ponderings.

Her hands paused as she stared at the crow's feet around her eyes. Anyone who'd lived long enough to have wrinkles had unpleasant memories of hurtful times. "I suppose everyone has things from their past they'd rather forget."

She pulled out the rest of her hairpins and picked up a maple-handled hairbrush. Pulling the brush slowly through her hair, she stared at her reflection in the oval mirror. Truth be told, Hubert wasn't the first to make her an offer of marriage since she became a widow. Seven years ago a man had attempted to court her while neglecting to mention he was already married. The very recollection made her sigh with the desire to erase not only the memory, but also the distrust that lingered from the experience.

She brushed a bit harder and pushed the dark image of the former would-be suitor from her mind. "And just because—it doesn't mean—" She drew her lips into a tight line, annoyed with her own thoughts. "Hubert has never been anything but a perfect Christian gentleman. I have no reason to imagine he could be deceitful about his past." She narrowed her eyes at her reflection. "He's told me about his first marriage, and I believe him."

She gathered her hair over one shoulder, and her fingers began deftly twisting it into a braid. "Lord, Your ways are far above my understanding. I trust You, Father. My heart is overflowing with happiness that the path You've designed for me includes Hubert."

She changed into her nightgown and robe, and sat in the old rocker with her Bible in her lap. "Father, the plain truth is I love Hubert, and because of my love for him, I want him to be happy. Thank You that You're bringing him and Everett back together after so many years. It fills me with joy to see his happiness. I pray that You will bless our marriage, and if it's Your will, let Everett come to Willow Creek so he and Hubert can be reunited."

※

Hubert stirred honey into his tea and crossed the room to sit beside the fireplace. Despite the mild temperature, he wanted the comfort of a fire. He stared into the flickering fingers that wrapped around the logs while guilt gnawed at him. Telling Pearl he had a headache wasn't entirely true. Oh, he had a headache now, but it wasn't the real reason he'd taken an early leave this evening. The annoying pain in his brow was born of regret.

When they were writing the letter to Everett, Pearl had assumed his hesitation about inviting his son to the wedding was because of their long estrangement and the uncertainty of Everett's reaction to the marriage. His heart pulled in opposite directions. His arms ached to embrace his son again. So much time—time he could never reclaim—had slipped away, and the father's heart that beat within him longed for reconciliation. Every letter that arrived from Everett flooded him with joy. Reuniting with his son was an answer to many years of prayer.

On the other hand, the one person in the world who knew why Hubert's wife left him was his son. If Everett came to Willow Creek for the wedding, would he disclose the details of that doomed marriage to Pearl? He'd felt like a fraud telling Everett in the letter that he was anxious to introduce him to Pearl. Perhaps he should rewrite the letter.

Reaching into his pocket, he extracted the envelope addressed to his son. The personal note Pearl had written was at the bottom of the last page—the same page that included his invitation for Everett to come to the wedding. He gazed at the graceful script of Pearl's hand. Sick in his heart, he slowly crumpled the page and tossed it into the fireplace and watched the flame consume it.

He stood and picked up his teacup and carried it across the room to the desk in the corner. Hubert uncovered the pot of ink and tapped his pen on the edge. Struggling to find the right words, he dipped the pen into the ink and carefully rewrote the last page, noting that he'd understand if Everett couldn't come to the wedding.

"Ah, Lord, I've learned over and over that even if one is forgiven a transgression, the consequences remain." He closed his eyes and leaned back against the oak desk chair. God had blessed him on so many sides, but this thorn festered in his flesh. He never dreamed God would give him another woman to love, but doing so created a paradox. Reuniting with Everett fulfilled one longing of his heart, but it also ran the risk of

Pearl learning of his past sins. If only he'd listened when God spoke all those years ago—if only he'd heeded God's direction. But being young and ambitious, he'd allowed the dream of success to blind him.

He took a sip of tea and discovered it had grown cold—just like his relationship with God had grown cold years ago. He'd long been comforted by the forgiveness God graciously bestowed and was diligent to never again permit the lure of worldly desires and aspirations to divide him from his loving heavenly Father. But the mistakes made during the broken fellowship could not be changed.

He returned to the fireplace and picked up the poker and prodded the logs, encouraging the flames to devour them. How he wished he could do the same with the regrets that had haunted him for twenty years. The loneliness that shadowed him for so long cast a reminder of the price of his disobedience. Sinking once again into the comfortable chair, he studied the blazing logs and pictured the sweet face of his intended.

"Pearl, my love, I want to be completely honest with you, but to do so, I have to admit that my failed marriage to Lucinda was the result of my selfishness and greed." Not exactly what a bride wanted to hear from her groom.

# four

Hubert engaged in mortal combat with the grime tracked from the street and up the steps in front of the mercantile. Using his broom, he attacked the miniature cloud of dust that billowed across the boardwalk and back down the steps. Impatience drove him as he slung the dirt back where it belonged. The activity served to work off some of the frustration of waiting to make Pearl his bride. Almost three weeks had passed since they'd written Everett telling him of their plans, and he and Pearl had still not decided on a specific date for the wedding. Since posting a FOR SALE sign on the front porch of the boardinghouse and sending advertisements for publication in several newspapers in the larger cities, they'd not received a single inquiry. He swiped the broom at one last spot of dirt and clomped back up the steps, dragging his grumpy disposition with him.

Two ladies with market baskets over their arms followed him in the door and he served them with his customary politeness, but the contentment he normally enjoyed operating the mercantile had vanished. He measured a length of cloth for one of the women and forced a smile as she looked over his supply of threads.

"Hubert!" Pearl bustled in the door. "Mrs. Russell just received a letter from her nephew and she said—" Pearl halted abruptly. "Oh, I'm sorry. I didn't realize you had customers. Good morning, Pamela, Christine."

The women chatted a moment with Pearl while Hubert gritted his teeth behind a pasted-on smile. His customers finally bid them both a good day and exited. He turned to

Pearl. Her blue eyes danced like those of a young girl.

"You were saying?"

"I couldn't wait to tell you." She set her reticule down on the counter. "You remember I told you I had spoken with Mrs. Russell about taking over the cooking and cleaning at the boardinghouse in exchange for free rent and a small salary—just until we can find a buyer." Words bubbled out of Pearl like water from a spring. She clasped her hands as if holding them in check. "Mrs. Russell corresponded with her nephew, the one who sends her money each month. He thinks it's fine if she wants to perform the duties, as long as she doesn't overtax herself."

Hubert's tentative smile beamed into a full-blown grin. "Does this mean we don't have to wait until the boardinghouse is sold before we can set a date?" His earlier grumpiness ebbed away like a vapor.

Pearl's laughter sounded like music. "That's what it means."

Hubert didn't hesitate another second. He grabbed Pearl, picked her up, and whirled her around, her skirts billowing like a sail in full tailwind.

"Hubert! Put me down! Mercy sakes! You're going to hurt yourself."

Hubert plunked her back on the floor, warmth creeping up his neck. Never before had he acted in such a demonstrative fashion. What in the world had gotten into him? Pearl clutched one hand to her chest and stared at him, speechless.

He tilted his head and gave her a sheepish grin. "I apologize, my dear, but your news has just made my day. No, my entire week." He took both her hands in his. As they locked gazes, a warm thrill rushed through him. He could hardly believe God had blessed him with such a wonderful woman. The idea of living out the remainder of his days with Pearl kicked his pulse up a notch. They shared a special smile—communicating more with a silent look than a thousand words could tell.

A hint of her lilac water teased his senses, and it was all he could do to keep from hanging the CLOSED sign on the door and running off with his intended to find the preacher that very minute.

He tucked her hand in the crook of his elbow and walked her to the door. The cheery red color of the flowers on her dress competed with the roses in her cheeks. His heart leaped within his chest, and he thanked God again that Pearl had said yes.

Hubert couldn't keep from smiling. "We need to discuss our plans."

Pearl's eyes twinkled. "Thinking about wedding plans makes me feel a bit giddy. Am I being foolish?"

He patted her hand. "If you are, then I'm foolish as well, because wedding plans have occupied a good portion of my thoughts."

She glanced up and down the boardwalk and lowered her voice. "Hubert, please don't think me selfish, but I'd rather have a small, quiet ceremony, something simple. Would you be terribly disappointed if we did that?"

A deep chuckle bubbled up from his middle. "Of course I wouldn't be disappointed." He leaned slightly forward. "The truth is I've been a little nervous about having a fancy wedding with all the trappings. Small and simple is fine with me."

Several doors down the street, the stage pulled up at the depot. Hubert glanced at his pocket watch and nodded. "Right on time. I always know when it's eleven o'clock, even if I've left my watch at home." He clicked the timepiece closed and slipped it back into his pocket. "Pastor Witherspoon usually goes home for lunch around noon, so we might stop by his house and ask him what day he can perform the ceremony."

Pearl nodded. "I'd like that just fine."

"Perhaps you'd like to have lunch at—"

The words caught in Hubert's throat. A single passenger disembarked the stage. The young man brushed dust from his coat and turned to reach up for his bag. Even at the distance between them, Hubert couldn't mistake the man's features.

"Hubert? What is it?" Concern colored Pearl's tone.

His mouth fell slightly agape, and he took a couple steps forward. Could it be?

"Everett?"

Hubert's feet moved of their own volition, and within seconds he was striding toward the stage depot. "Everett? Son?"

The young man halted and looked up. Recognition lit his eyes, and he set his bag on the boardwalk. "Father."

The two clasped hands in a strong handshake, and Hubert pulled his son into an embrace. Joy spilled over him in bucketfuls. Hubert clapped his son on the back, then grasped him by both shoulders.

"Son, I can hardly believe you're here." Emotion burned behind his eyes. Everett—his boy—had actually come to see him. How many years of regret passed between them, wasted years like water slipping through his fingers? But he held the answer to his prayers in his arms.

"It's so good to see you, son."

"It's good to finally be here." The timbre of Everett's voice carried the unmistakable ring of maturity—deeper, stronger. His firm, square jaw, inherited from his grandfather, was more pronounced now that manhood etched its mark over Everett's features. Adolescence had been left behind. When did that happen?

Everett glanced around, as if giving the town a cursory appraisal. His eyebrows dipped, drawn together by small lines above the bridge of his nose. Another family resemblance left its imprint on the boy—not a physical trait, but rather in his mannerisms. A hint of arrogance. "So this is Willow Creek."

Hubert's detective instincts kicked in without effort. If he didn't miss his guess, his son was less than impressed by the town. A tiny twist pinched his gut. Everett's arrival caught him by surprise, something that rarely happened. A sensation akin to anxiety swept through him. How many weeks and months had he dreamed of this day? Now that he stood face-to-face with his son, he wished he'd had more notice, more time to prepare.

"Hubert? Is this your son?"

He spun around. Pearl stood a few steps behind him, waiting to be introduced.

☙

Pearl's heart accelerated in a rush of joy. What a blessing to witness Hubert's reunion with his son! She stepped forward, side by side with Hubert.

Hubert placed his hand on her shoulder. "Son, I'd like you to meet Pearl Dunnigan. Pearl, this is my son, Everett Behr."

Everett extended his hand. Pearl accepted his offer of a handshake. His brown eyes darkened as they scrutinized her face. Stiffness drew his shoulders back. "Mrs. Dunnigan."

Her breath hesitated. The formality of his tone and stately air gave her pause. Perhaps his upbringing in a wealthy home instilled the reserved manners and propriety. Regardless, he stood waiting for her response.

"It–it's so good to finally meet you, Ev—uh, Mr. Behr." She couldn't remember the last time she felt so awkward meeting a person.

Everett cast a cool glance over her and returned his attention to his father. "I made my travel arrangements as soon as I received your last letter."

Hubert smiled, but it wasn't the warm smile Pearl was accustomed to seeing.

"I'm so happy you could come, son. In fact, Pearl and I were just discussing the wedding." Hubert bent to retrieve

Everett's bag. "You must be tired and hungry after your trip. Let's get you settled. We'll have plenty of time to talk later."

Everett nodded and without so much as a glance in Pearl's direction, he replied to his father. "Is there a hotel here?"

Hubert chuckled. "Hotel? Yes we have a hotel, but I'd rather hoped you'd want to stay with me." He extended his arm to Pearl, gesturing for her to join them.

"Um, Hubert?" Pearl reached out to touch his sleeve. "Excuse me for interrupting, but since it's only a little after eleven o'clock, you can't close the store right now. Why don't I take Everett to the boardinghouse? He can relax and refresh himself, and I can make sure he has a hearty lunch. After he rests, you can take him to your house."

A flash of something foreign darted through Hubert's eyes—an indescribable emotion she'd never seen on his face before. He appeared to hedge a moment, trying to form a response. Before he could reply to her offer, however, Everett spoke.

"Thank you, Mrs. Dunnigan. I'm sure you mean well, but I think it best if I remain with my father." He turned away from her, and she felt an air of dismissal. "Father, surely you have employees who can operate your enterprise in your absence."

Pearl's mouth dropped open at Everett's cold reaction to her invitation. Did Hubert notice his son's rudeness? To her surprise, Hubert hurriedly agreed with Everett.

"It's no problem to close the store for the remainder of the day."

"But Hubert, your customers—"

"Will simply have to come back tomorrow." He started up the boardwalk with Everett on one side of him and Pearl hastening her steps to keep up with him on the other. "This is a special occasion. My son has arrived for a visit."

They stopped at the mercantile so Hubert could hang

the CLOSED sign and lock the doors. Pearl stood to one side, unsure if Hubert even remembered she was there. Determined not to dampen his joy over Everett's arrival, she waited quietly for him to share his plans.

Hubert dropped the store key in his pocket and turned a broad grin on his son. "Now, we have the rest of the day to spend catching up with each other."

When Hubert finally turned to her, the warmth had returned to his eyes. "Pearl, my dear, why don't you join us? We can have an early lunch at the hotel and then take Everett to my place."

At his mention of the hotel, her spirits dipped a bit. Hubert always loved her thick roast beef sandwiches and potato salad, and she'd made an applesauce cake just that morning.

"I'd still like to make lunch for both of you at the boardinghouse." She slid her gaze between father and son. "But you are entirely correct, Hubert. This is a special occasion. Whatever you want to do is fine with me."

Everett's frown made her feel like an intruder. Was she being presumptuous? Of course he probably wanted his father to himself, at least for the first day of his visit. She could understand that. But before she could voice her thoughts, Hubert took her hand and tucked it within the crook of his arm.

"Since I'm taking the day off, you should, too." His smile calmed her mounting apprehension. "Join us for lunch, then I'll get Everett settled at my house."

They crossed the street and entered the hotel dining room, but when Hubert held her chair as she was seated, Everett's glower caught her attention. Her smile fell from her face. She wasn't imagining it. Everett resented her presence.

"So Father, I'm a bit confused." Everett scooted his chair closer to the table. "You have no employees trustworthy enough to run your establishment while you're away? Closing the place doesn't seem prudent."

Hubert chuckled. "I am my only employee. I suppose at some point I should consider hiring someone to work part-time." He smiled across the table at Pearl. "Especially after the wedding."

Her stomach normally danced with delight at Hubert's references to their upcoming nuptials, but Everett's apparent displeasure cast a pall on her happiness. She couldn't help but wonder why he'd come. At first, she assumed his intention was to reunite with his father and share in the joy of the wedding. Now she wasn't so sure. What if she didn't pass muster as his father's future wife? Is that why he was here? To inspect the woman who was about to marry his father?

She silently admonished herself for her undisciplined imagination. *Don't be silly. After receiving the letter Hubert and I wrote together, telling him about our marriage plans, of course he'd want to come and celebrate with us. Hubert invited him to come. He's simply tired from his journey.* She returned her attention to the conversation between the two men, only to discover them both training expectant gazes upon her.

"Pearl?" Hubert's eyes studied her with concern.

Heat rose from her middle and filled her face. "I'm sorry. I wasn't paying attention. That was rude of me."

Everett cleared his throat and arched his eyebrows. "I asked you if you operate the town boardinghouse."

"Why, yes." She took a sip from her water glass. "I've been running the boardinghouse for many years, ever since my husband died."

"I see." Everett's chin rose slightly. "What kind of people stay at a boardinghouse?"

She wasn't sure she understood his question. What was Everett's point in asking? Did he think she operated a house of ill repute?

"Everett." Annoyance seeped through Hubert's voice at his son's inquiry. "Pearl runs a respectable establishment."

"Of course she does." There was no remorse in his tone, nor was an apology forthcoming. "I merely wondered if the clients she served are dependent upon her charity or if they contribute to society in any way."

Pearl couldn't have been more surprised if Everett had tossed the contents of his water glass in her face. There was no mistaking the disdain in the young man's voice. Whatever Hubert's answer was, it didn't register in her mind.

The waitress brought their food, and Hubert asked the blessing. Pearl picked at her plate, glancing up at Hubert from time to time. An uncomfortable lapse in conversation ensued, and Pearl got the distinct impression Everett had things he wished to discuss with Hubert, but not in her presence. By the time they finished their meal, Pearl couldn't remember what she ate. They rose to leave, and Hubert paid for their lunch.

Once outside on the boardwalk, he turned to Everett. "Will you excuse us a moment, son?"

Without waiting for Everett's reply, Hubert gently guided her a few steps away. "I'm so sorry, my dear. Once he is settled at the house, I intend to have a talk with him and let him know I didn't approve of the way he spoke to you." He gave her elbow a little squeeze. "For now, may I see you back to the boardinghouse on our way home?"

The warmth of Hubert's hand on her arm gave her spirit reassurance. "No, I still have a couple of errands to run." She risked a quick glance in Everett's direction and found him scowling. "I'd like for the two of you to come to dinner, if you have no other plans."

Hubert sucked in a breath. "I think it will probably be best if Everett and I spend the evening at my house. We have some things to discuss. May I stop by the boardinghouse in the morning on my way to the store?"

"Of course. I'll have fresh coffee ready."

He squeezed her fingers and said good-bye. Though her heart felt a certain amount of vindication that Hubert intended to confront Everett about the way the young man had behaved, she couldn't push away the distress. Nor could she forget the expression on Everett's face when Hubert introduced him to her. Her own words echoed in her mind as she made her way down the boardwalk.

*You mustn't let anything stand in the way of reconciling with your son.*

Hubert's response to her encouragement that initially prompted joy now resounded like a dirge. *I don't intend to.*

## *five*

Hubert fought a tug-of-war with his emotions as he studied his cup of tea and waited for Everett to finish unpacking and join him. From their first embrace at the stage depot, Everett's demeanor had reminded him of the young man's grandmother—condescending and haughty. He hoped Everett's churlishness was simply due to travel fatigue. He shook his head. Why did his joy over being reunited with his son have to be dampened?

A discordant duet played in his mind. Everett's arrival was a surprise. It had pained Hubert to toss the last page of the letter he and Pearl had written together into the fire—grieved him to watch the flames destroy the invitation to the wedding. How could a man be so torn in such distinctly opposite directions? For years, his heart had longed for reconciliation with Everett. But Everett's knowledge of Hubert's past choices made him the one person Hubert didn't want to introduce to Pearl. He thought removing the invitation from the letter was enough.

But Everett chose to come. Judging by his son's attitude thus far, celebration didn't seem to be his purpose for traveling halfway across the country.

Hubert reprimanded his thoughts and sipped his tea. "Drop the investigator posture, Behr. You're not a Pinkerton any longer."

"Did you say something, Father?" Everett entered the room and sat in the leather chair across from Hubert.

Hubert forced a smile. "Just talking to myself. It's one of the hazards of living alone."

Everett's fingers curled around the arms of the chair as he sent a slow, surveying scan around the room. Even though Hubert had indulged in several luxuries when he'd built the house, no doubt Everett considered it rustic. Why, surely the spacious front sitting room with its river rock fireplace and colorful woven rugs could never be deemed a proper parlor by Everett's standards. After living in affluence for so many years, would his son consider the house inferior? But Everett's opinion of the house wasn't what burdened Hubert.

Hubert gestured to the teapot and extra cup sitting on the low table between them. "Would you like some tea? It's Earl Grey."

His son raised one eyebrow. "So you do enjoy a few genteel things out here in this. . .wilderness."

Hubert's heart pinched. His detective skills were still as sharp as ever. His son indeed viewed the town with contempt. A breath of defensiveness rose in his chest, but he pushed it back.

"It's hardly a wilderness. I've found I rather enjoy the quiet life here in Willow Creek. There is a serenity in the surroundings one can't experience in the noise of the city."

Everett snorted as he poured himself a cup of tea. "There's a great many things one can't experience in a backwoods hamlet that the city affords. Culture, society, conveniences, sophistication. . ." He stirred a spoonful of sugar into his cup and took a tentative sip.

Debating the advantages of the city with those of rural Iowa wasn't what Hubert wished to discuss. "I know your grandparents provided you a higher standard of living than that to which the good people of Willow Creek are accustomed. However, I would ask that you demonstrate a bit more graciousness. It so happens that I love this little town and its residents."

Everett's expression darkened, and he set his cup on his saucer. "My apologies, Father. Reverend Werner suggested I try to employ more understanding and compassion of others."

"Reverend Werner?"

"Yes, he was the minister who came regularly to see Grandfather. I believe he pastored a small church on the other side of town." Everett set his cup and saucer on the table. "At first I was a bit taken aback. The minister from the largest church in Baltimore where we attended for years never came to the house, even when Grandmother died. When Grandfather took ill, Reverend Werner started coming to visit. I never did learn how Grandfather met him."

Hubert ran his finger around the rim of his cup. "This Reverend Werner—did he come often?"

A shadow flicked over Everett's face, followed by a slight raise of his chin. "He came every week, mostly to talk with Grandfather, but whenever Grandfather was asleep, Reverend Werner would sit and talk to me. He spoke of Jesus like a best Friend rather than a distant entity."

"Did this man preach your grandfather's funeral?"

"Yes." Everett sat forward and his expression took on a hint of animation. "He said Grandfather knew Jesus in a personal way. It was most comforting to hear him talk about heaven, and how those he called 'believers' could one day go there."

Hubert's heart leaped. "Did you make the decision to believe?"

Everett leaned back in the chair and hesitated for a minute. "You know, I kept telling myself it was nonsense— nothing more than a comforting story a minister might tell to a dying man. But I must admit the different passages Reverend Werner suggested I study raised some questions in my mind."

Joy filled Hubert's soul, but before he could inquire further about his son's possible faith, Everett abruptly changed the subject.

"So tell me, Father, when did you first meet Mrs. Dunnigan?"

Once again caught off guard, Hubert covered his hesitation by taking another sip of his barely warm tea. He'd wait for God to supply another opportunity to talk to Everett about his faith.

After briefly filling Everett in on the details of his last Pinkerton case that brought him to Willow Creek two years earlier, he leveled his gaze at his son. "I realized several months ago that I was falling in love with Pearl. That might sound strange coming from someone my age, but I am quite certain God brought me to Willow Creek for the purpose of meeting the woman I would eventually marry."

Cynicism crept into Everett's expression. "Really, Father. The woman runs a boardinghouse."

Hubert bristled, but he held himself in restraint. Nothing would be gained by allowing his passion to take control of the situation. Instead, he purposely modulated his voice. "There is certainly nothing wrong with running a boardinghouse. But since you brought it up, I must say I didn't appreciate the tone you took with Pearl at lunch or the attitude you displayed when you posed your questions to her. Pearl Dunnigan is a fine, hardworking Christian woman, and the boardinghouse she runs has an excellent reputation."

Almost a full minute of silence passed while Everett turned his gaze toward the window. When he returned his vision to Hubert, scorn twisted his lips. "Father, I happen to know the Pinkerton Detective Agency pays its investigators quite well. You even mentioned in one of your letters that your retirement bonus was a rather tidy sum."

Hubert wasn't sure he followed Everett's line of reasoning. What did his Pinkerton salary or his retirement bonus have to do with Pearl's boardinghouse? His confusion must have shown on his face because Everett arched one eyebrow and tipped his head toward the window that overlooked the edge of town.

"I suspect this woman is—"

"Her name is Pearl." The muscles in Hubert's neck tensed, but he forced his tone to remain even. "When you speak to her or refer to her, please do so respectfully."

Everett's eyes narrowed but he didn't retort. Instead, he appeared to take a deep breath—whether to sigh in resignation or calm himself, Hubert couldn't tell.

"All right, I will be respectful. But Father, I can't help but feel you are marrying beneath you. Mrs. Dunnigan likely doesn't make a great deal of money running a boardinghouse for people who can't afford a home of their own." He paused before making his point. "Have you considered that she might be seeking a marriage of comfort and position?"

The tightness in Hubert's neck extended to his jaw muscles. He clenched and unclenched his fingers. Allowing his temper to erupt would not only destroy the fragile relationship between him and Everett, it would also negate any chance to speak of his faith with his son. He certainly didn't want to start out by setting parameters, but he couldn't allow Everett to voice such speculations about Pearl. Distress burned in his chest. Unless Everett changed his attitude, the possibility loomed of having to make a choice between his son and the woman he loved.

He pulled in a deep breath and gentled his response. "Everett, I can't describe how happy I am that you have come to visit." It wasn't a lie. He was both overjoyed and alarmed. "I've prayed for years that the wrongs of the past could be made right between us, that you might forgive me for the mistakes I made when you were a child, and we might begin to enjoy being father and son." He nailed Everett with an unblinking stare. "But this you must understand: I love Pearl, and she loves me. What we share is a gift given by God. We both feel God is blessing our plans for marriage." He took another steadying breath as the knot in his stomach tightened. "Son, I cannot tolerate derogatory statements about Pearl's character. She is going to be my wife."

Thick uneasiness pervaded the space between them, and for a minute Hubert was afraid Everett might go and purchase a ticket for the next eastbound stage.

Finally, Everett gave a slight nod. "As you wish, Father. I was merely wondering if Mrs. Dunnigan was an appropriate match for my father, but it seems you have already made up your mind. As I recall, once you set yourself to do something, there is nothing that can sway you."

Hubert realized Everett's statement had little to do with his plans to marry Pearl. He dropped his gaze to his teacup. The remaining beverage in the cup was now cold, much like Everett's words.

"Son, if I could live my life over, there are a lot of things I'd do differently." He shifted his jaw back and forth, despising the admission of guilt he knew he needed to offer to Everett, and asking God for the grace to do so. "In hindsight, I can now see that taking cases that kept me on the road for weeks, and sometimes months, was not the choice I should have made. My place was at home with you and your mother. Perhaps. . .perhaps if I'd allowed God's wisdom instead of my ambition to drive me, you might not have grown up without your parents."

Silence as oppressive as the July heat filled the room and hung there like an impenetrable fog. Voicing the admission of guilt put him in a vulnerable position. He wasn't saying anything Everett didn't already know, but the words had to pass between them before a bridge could be built. He blew out a pent-up breath and continued.

"Your grandparents were good people and even though they

gave you a fine home, I regret leaving you there for them to raise. I should have been the one to influence and teach you as you grew. I'm asking you to forgive me for not being the father I should have been."

Everett's gaze remained lowered, but he blinked several times. "We both have regrets, Father. Mine is that I allowed Grandmother to poison my mind against you."

Hubert shook his head. "You were only a child. If I'd been a better husband and father, you wouldn't have grown up in your grandparents' house." There were other regrets, but none that he felt comfortable sharing with his son, especially not on the first day of his visit.

Everett stifled a yawn behind his hand. "I'm rather tired. If it's all right with you, I think I'll lie down for a while." He rose and went to his room, leaving Hubert alone with his tangled thoughts. Ironic how he was able to give voice to the remorse he felt over his past mistakes, but he couldn't bring himself to sit down with Pearl and tell her the same thing. So many what-ifs and if onlys.

"If only. . ." He closed his eyes and rested his head against the leather back of the chair. The fact that Everett hadn't responded to his plea for forgiveness wasn't lost on Hubert. How strange that God was so quick to forgive him, but his son withheld that which God gave freely. He gave a huff of resignation. He couldn't condemn Everett for his lack of forgiveness. After all, despite God's outpouring of pardon the moment he'd asked, he had yet to forgive himself.

❧

"I'd never forgive myself if I came between Hubert and his son." Pearl punched her fist into the soft blob of bread dough on the kitchen worktable.

Tessa set her coffee mug down with a *thunk*. "That's ridiculous. Why would you think something like that?"

Pearl's shoulders drooped with a sigh. "It's clear Everett

doesn't like me. I felt like an interloper sitting at lunch with them. If I could have thought of a clever way to excuse myself, I'd have left them alone, but I suppose I was just so stunned. . . ." She left the thought unfinished and returned her energy to kneading the dough.

"Stunned?" Tessa dipped her head and tilted it at an angle so Pearl couldn't help catching her wide-eyed look.

She wished she could simply shrug off the angst that sent a chill through her every time the expression on Everett's face came to mind. The memory of his disdain sent darts of foreboding through her.

"I suppose I don't measure up to Everett's expectations." She separated the dough into four equal portions and placed each one in a pan. After lining the pans up on the warming shelf above the stove, she turned and wiped her hands on her apron. "I don't think Everett approves of his father marrying me."

A frown pinched Tessa's brow. "Why not?"

Pearl sat opposite her friend. With her elbows on the table, she clasped her hands and rested her chin on her closed fingers. "I'm not sure, but I think he feels I'm not good enough for Hubert."

An explosion of air sputtered from Tessa's lips. "He obviously doesn't know you. You and Hubert are a perfect match. Neither one of you would be complete without the other." The young woman pressed her palms down on the table. "What did Hubert tell him?"

Pearl forced a tight smile and shrugged. "Hubert stopped by this morning for coffee on his way to the mercantile, like he always does. He told me that he and Everett talked some yesterday afternoon." She rose and checked the heat in the oven. "He seems to think Everett will come around." She added a couple more pieces of split stove wood to the firebox.

"Meanwhile. . ." Pearl placed her hands on her hips as she turned back to Tessa. "I suppose I'll just see what God has in store. I don't know what else to do." She returned to her chair and reached across the table to wrap her fingers around those of the young woman who was as dear to her as a daughter. "Mercy sakes, I don't know what to do, Tessa. What if Everett is so set against me being his father's wife that he talks Hubert into breaking our engagement?" Tightness in her throat caused her words to come out in a croak.

Moisture glinted in Tessa's eyes, and she covered Pearl's hands with hers. "I seem to remember a time when I asked you questions along the same line. I was so confused about my feelings for Gideon. The idea of being in love with a man scared me to death. So I came and talked it over with the wisest woman I know." She gave Pearl's fingers a tug. "And you know what she told me?"

Pearl blinked a tear away. "Now I suppose you're going to feed me my own words?"

A grin tipped Tessa's lips. "The advice you gave me was to seek God and ask Him to guide me."

Pearl pulled back one hand and rubbed her forehead. "Tessa, I feel like I'm riding both sides of the seesaw in the schoolyard. Not only am I afraid Everett might insist his father break the engagement, there is another side to this." Needle pricks of agitation stung the back of her neck, and she couldn't remain seated. Leaving her chair, she paced to the window and stared out through the red gingham-checked curtains to the hollyhocks in the backyard.

She swallowed hard. "Of course I'll seek God's guidance. But I can't come between Hubert and his son. I can't. Hubert has prayed for this reunion for so long."

Behind her, she heard chair legs scrape the floor and Tessa's soft footsteps closing the distance between them. Her friend's arms slipped around her shoulders, and her soft voice nudged Pearl to face the question she'd been avoiding.

"What does your heart tell you?"

*six*

"So I got to thinking. . ." Pearl tilted her head to one side, seeking Hubert's approval of her plan. "Perhaps if the two of you came to the boardinghouse for dinner tomorrow night, we could get better acquainted."

After turning the situation over in her mind for three days, Pearl had risen much earlier than normal and spent time asking God to reveal His will to her. By the time she'd put breakfast on the table for her boarders, the Old Testament scripture in Isaiah echoed through her mind: *Come now, and let us reason together. . . .* Sitting down together over dinner simply made sense. She'd spent many years serving people at her table and found most folks more amiable after a satisfying meal. She'd impatiently watched for Hubert to stick his head in the back door, as was his habit every morning.

Now her heart fluttered as a tender expression softened Hubert's eyes and a smile creased his face. "Ah, Pearl, my love, you always know the right thing to do. That's a splendid idea."

Pearl glanced beyond his shoulder to see if any of the boarders heard his expression of endearment.

He drained his coffee cup and carried it to the dishpan, then paused, a twinkle in his eye. "Might I talk you into making your special pot roast?"

Delight skittered up Pearl's spine. "Pot roast it is." Hope swelled in her chest. "Do you really think Everett will be receptive to the idea?"

Hubert retrieved his hat from the peg by the door. "I'll talk to him about it when I see him this evening." He caught her hand and brushed a soft kiss across her fingers. "Once he gets to know you, I'm sure he'll understand why I fell in love with you. Dining together is a perfect way to start."

She gave Hubert's fingers a gentle tug. "Hubert, I'm so happy that he has come all this way to attend the wedding."

A brief shadow flicked across Hubert's face. Everett's arrival revealed a strain she'd not seen before in Hubert's eyes. No doubt he couldn't help but be anxious over their reunion. She prayed her dinner plans would help ease the tension.

"I'm happy he's here as well." A tiny twitch of the space between his brows, however, pricked Pearl with wonder. She wasn't accustomed to seeing him nervous about anything. His uneasiness underscored how important this reconciliation was to him. Her determination to see Hubert happy doubled.

Hubert departed for the mercantile and Pearl began cleaning the kitchen, but her mind wasn't on her task. Everything about this dinner had to be perfect, from the main course to the dessert. But one thing niggled at her. How could Everett and Hubert feel relaxed and converse freely with four boarders sitting at the table scrutinizing them?

"That will never do," she muttered to herself as she plunged dishes into the hot soapy water and pondered how to create a comfortable atmosphere. Vexation rubbed a raw spot on her heart, and she remembered Tessa's encouragement to seek God. "Father, I know this idea came from You. So You're going to have to help me with the planning."

The menu was easy; she'd make all Hubert's favorites, starting with the pot roast.

When she turned to wipe the worn kitchen worktable, she halted. Glancing around the cheerful kitchen, an idea began to take shape.

Pearl smoothed her best tablecloth over the kitchen worktable, concealing the scarred surface. A bouquet of summer flowers in a glass vase adorned the center of the table while the tantalizing aroma of roasting beef and vegetables filled the room. Two plump, golden-crusted apple pies sat on the warming shelf of the stove. She was grateful her understanding boarders didn't mind her not sitting with them in the dining room tonight, and she'd spent the day fussing to make the intimate confines of the kitchen as festive and inviting as possible.

She tapped her chin with one finger as she studied the table. Would candles be too formal? The kerosene lamp that hung over the table, along with the two wall lamps, would afford enough light, but candles might lend an air of graciousness. She scurried to the breakfront in the dining room to fetch the candlesticks that had belonged to her mother.

After polishing the candlesticks to make them sparkle, she arranged them on the table and stepped back to inspect the finished layout. She was pleased with the result of her efforts, but hers wasn't the opinion that counted. Another prayer winged heavenward from her lips for a successful evening.

She glanced at the clock and hurried to her room to change her dress. Hubert and Everett were due to arrive in a half hour, and she wanted to serve her boarders first so she'd be free to sit and enjoy the evening. A pinch of apprehension caused her heart to skip.

Her hands shook as she unpinned and rearranged her hair. "Oh, mercy sakes, Pearl, stop behaving like a silly goose." She berated her image in the oval mirror. The memory of getting ready for her first dinner with Hubert tiptoed through her mind, and she smiled at the fond recollection. The upturn of her lips faded into a rueful grimace as a thought settled into the pit of her stomach. This was different. Her anticipation of the coming evening wasn't filled with schoolgirl flutters but rather a sense of foreboding.

She scurried to put the boarders' dinner on the dining room table. Pearl left them to ask the blessing and pass the food around while she returned to the kitchen to recheck every detail.

The roast was ready, and butter swam in the indentations of the potatoes mounded in Pearl's favorite china bowl. Glazed carrots and fresh green beans sat on the warming shelf above the stove. She peeked into the oven at the rolls. A rap at the front door made her catch her breath. She smoothed her skirt and touched her hair as she bustled to open the door.

"Good evening, Hubert, Everett. Please come in." She stepped aside to allow the two men to enter. Hubert gave her a stealthy wink and she smiled in return. But when she turned to welcome Everett and take his hat, his contemptuous frown seared her tattered shreds of hope.

"I–I'm so g–glad you could come, Everett."

"The pleasure's all mine, I'm sure." Everett's sweeping gaze took in the entry hall and the doorway that led to the dining room where the voices of the boarders and clinking of silverware on china indicated dinner was already underway. He took a step in that direction, but Pearl spoke up quickly.

"Hubert, I thought it would be nice if we'd have this time to ourselves." She sent him a pleading look to beg for his support. "So I set up the kitchen table for us. We can have our dinner and talk in privacy there."

Hubert slipped her arm through the crook of his elbow. "A fine idea, my dear. And dinner smells wonderful, doesn't it, son?"

Pearl nearly wilted in relief at Hubert's encouraging agreement, but when Everett stopped and turned to look over his shoulder at her, his scathing glare left no doubt as to his opinion, even before he opened his mouth.

"We're eating in the kitchen?" The young man pulled his stare away from Pearl and flung it at his father.

Pearl's feet felt nailed to the floor, but thankfully Hubert didn't miss a beat. "The kitchen is fine, and I've brought my appetite. Is that your special pot roast I smell?" He started down the hall toward the kitchen with Pearl on his arm, bypassing the dining room.

She almost reminded him that he'd requested pot roast, but realized he was covering her nervousness by making the observation. "Yes, I knew it was your favorite. Just let me take the rolls out of the oven and we can sit down." She busied herself setting brimming bowls and the meat platter on the table, along with the rolls, browned to perfection.

"Why, it looks like a banquet hall in here," Hubert said as he held her chair. She placed a small bowl of butter next to the basket of rolls and sat across the table from Everett, thanking Hubert for his gentlemanly gesture. Too late, she realized her position would require her to look directly at Everett throughout the meal.

Hubert sat and offered the prayer while Pearl squeezed her hands together in her lap. She could feel Everett's cold stare, even with her head bowed. When Hubert said amen, she passed the sliced roast to him and the rolls to Everett.

"This looks magnificent, my dear." Hubert forked a generous portion of tender beef onto his plate and passed the platter to his son. "Everett, tell us about the new piers and shipping interests being built along the Patapsco River and Baltimore Harbor. Some of these enterprises will greatly boost the economy. Isn't that what you said, son?"

Pearl passed the bowl of carrots to Everett, who ignored the offering. When Everett didn't reply to his father, she glanced at Hubert, while still holding the bowl in limbo.

The young man's demeanor didn't seem any friendlier this evening, and he couldn't use travel fatigue as an excuse. She set the carrots down.

"Sounds fascinating." She lied, desperate to encourage conversation on any topic.

An indifferent sniff came from Everett's side of the table. "Really Father, I doubt Mrs. Dunnigan would care about Baltimore's commerce." A disdainful frown punctuated his features.

Hubert and Pearl exchanged glances. The evening had started out badly and was going downhill. Hubert mentioned a few new items he'd ordered for the mercantile, idle chat designed, Pearl suspected, to fill the cold silence.

Pearl's gaze slid in Everett's direction, and she found him scowling at his plate from which he'd barely eaten a bite. Perhaps preparing all Hubert's favorites had been a mistake. Should she have inquired as to Everett's preferences?

Finally, just as she was about to bring the apple pie and coffee to the table, Everett abruptly scraped his chair across the wooden plank floor and stood. "If you will excuse me. . ." He tossed his napkin on his plate and exited the kitchen.

Pearl started to rise. "But Everett—"

Hubert reached over and caught her arm. With a sigh, he closed his eyes. "Let him go, Pearl."

Pearl could barely keep her voice steady. "But I made apple pie for dessert." Her throat tightened. "Hubert, what did I do wrong?"

"You did nothing wrong." Hubert shook his head. "This is between Everett and me; things we still need to discuss to. . . clear the air."

They both rose and Hubert took her hand. "I'm sorry, my dear. You worked hard to make this evening special, and everything was lovely." He pulled her into a gentle hug and the comfort of his embrace eased the sting of Everett's rebuff.

Hubert cupped her chin. "I'm going to go talk to him, and then I'll be back. You keep a piece of that pie warm for me, all right?"

Tears burned the back of her eyes and a vise gripped her middle. All she could do was nod before Hubert let himself out the back door.

&

"Doesn't she know that servants eat in the kitchen?" Everett's arrogance rang in Hubert's ears. "I was insulted, as you should have been."

By the time Hubert caught up with Everett, his son had already crossed the threshold of Hubert's house. He clamped his teeth down on the anger he wanted to lash at his son. Instead, he pointed to a chair. "Sit down, son. There are some things we need to discuss."

Instead, Everett tromped across the room, then spun to face his father. "You know I'm right. Mrs. Dunnigan is hardly the type of woman you should be considering for a wife. I doubt there is anyone in this town suitable—"

"You're wrong, son. There is one person and I am engaged to her." Anger warred with compunction in his breast. "Your behavior tonight was completely unacceptable. I asked you before, now I'm telling you—you will treat Pearl with respect."

He rubbed his hand over his mouth and chin, shoved the other hand in his pocket, and took three steps toward the window. He could see the rooftop of the boardinghouse from his front window. Pearl must be distraught. She'd worked so hard on the preparations for the dinner, and it turned into a disaster.

An insolent huff sounded across the room as Everett continued pacing back and forth. "This isn't really about your engagement, is it, Father? This is about you doing whatever you want to do, no matter what anyone else thinks."

Hubert turned to face his son and saw contempt on Everett's face. "Son, there is no way I can turn the clock back and make the wrongs right again. I've told you how sorry I am, how much I regret the choices I made twenty years ago."

Everett turned his back on his father, not saying a word for a full minute. His shoulders rose and fell as if a great battle were taking place within. "How was I supposed to understand, Father? I was eight years old." When he turned, Hubert saw the sheen of tears in his son's eyes despite the shadows in the room. "I couldn't understand why my father was always gone, or why my mother left me at my grandparents' house and never came back. It was your fault Mother left, because you didn't care about anybody but yourself."

The words stung, but Hubert did nothing to stop the torrent. He pulled off his jacket and sat in one of the chairs facing the cold fireplace. This was the real reason Everett came. After so many years of bitterness building up in him, he wanted—no, he needed to spew it all out at his father. Hubert sat quietly and let his son rant.

When Everett finally ran out of accusations, he slumped in the chair across from his father. Hubert leaned forward. "Son, I'm sorry. I wish I could undo my past choices, but I can't. All I can do is love you right now, and pray you will one day find it in your heart to forgive me."

Everett raised his head, looking drained of the anger that initiated the tirade. The rage that burned in his eyes minutes before now smoldered into resignation. "In spite of everything, I finally realized that I love you, too. But knowing that just seemed to make me angrier." He pulled his tie off and loosened the top button of his shirt. "There are a lot of things I still don't understand, Father."

Hubert nodded. "My engagement to Pearl is one of those things, isn't it?"

"Yes." Everett lifted his chin and pointed a recriminating look at Hubert. "I know you don't want me speaking ill of her, but I still feel this engagement is wrong."

"Why?" Bewilderment dug a hole into Hubert's chest. "Is it because she doesn't have the social standing you and your grandparents were accustomed to? Because if that's your only objection to her, I can counter by describing her standing in this community."

Scorn lifted one corner of Everett's mouth, and before he could reply, Hubert went on. "Pearl Dunnigan is a fine Christian woman, loved by just about everyone in this town. No, Willow Creek isn't much compared to Baltimore, and we may not have a social register, but we have something better. We have a fellowship, a family of faith. Wealth, influence, and prestige aren't the means by which we measure a person's worth. We look at their character, integrity, compassion, the way they love others and serve God. Those are the qualities that make Pearl the woman I love. That, and the way she loves me."

Hubert sat back, waiting for Everett's retort, but it never came. Instead, his son pulled himself to his feet. "I apologize for ruining the evening. If it's all right with you, I believe I'll retire. Good night."

"Good night."

Hubert let his head fall back against the leather-covered upholstery and heaved a sigh. The bitterness Everett had carried for so many years was like an infection that needed to be lanced and drained. He could only pray that when the surgery was over, their relationship would be healed.

He picked up his jacket and started toward his room, only to stop short. He'd told Pearl he would be back. She'd be wondering where he was. He pulled out his pocket watch and squinted at the hands. It was past ten o'clock. He couldn't risk Pearl's reputation by knocking on her door at such a late hour.

"In the morning," he muttered to himself. "I'll stop by first thing and explain why I didn't go back." He shuffled to his bedroom. "Lord, please comfort Pearl tonight."

## *seven*

Dawn stained the eastern sky pink and gold as Hubert climbed the back porch steps of the boardinghouse. He tapped on the kitchen door before poking his head inside.

"May I come in, or are you angry that I didn't come back last night?"

Pearl closed the oven door and straightened. Her face reflected a combination of relief and anxiety. "Come in, Hubert. I'm not angry, but I was worried." She wiped her hands on her apron and poured him a cup of coffee. "Did you and Everett argue?" Lines creased her brow.

Hubert accepted the steaming brew and took a tentative sip. "I'm not sure one could call it an argument." He sat on the same chair he'd occupied hours before at dinner. "There are many issues Everett and I need to work through. The letter writing has opened the door, but painful things from the past still need to be addressed."

Pearl paused in the middle of cracking eggs into a bowl. "I don't understand. What does any of that have to do with me? It's as if he dislikes me for something I've done. . .or not done." She resumed cracking and beating the eggs. "What is it about me—"

"Nothing." Hubert quickly rose to close the space between them. "His behavior has nothing to do with you." He filled his lungs slowly and blew the air out. Was it a lie to tell Pearl that Everett carried no grudge against her? Regardless, Hubert refused to allow Pearl to blame herself for Everett's arrogance.

He took her hand and turned her to face him. Silver

strands of hair hugged her ears, begging his fingers to trace their path. Instead, he tipped her chin up and gently stroked her jawline with his thumb. "Pearl, please don't fret about this. Everett did a lot of talking last night, and I did a lot of listening. His anger and bitterness go back several years, long before I met you." He hoped his tone sounded reassuring.

Pearl's eyebrows dipped and her lips formed a tight, thin line. She shrugged and turned back to the stove. "It's not any of my business, but why is Everett so angry? You never really told me what happened between you that caused the rift." She glanced over her shoulder at him. "If you don't want to talk about it, I understand. I just thought you might find it easier to get it off your chest to me, since I'm not the one who's angry."

Her offer of a listening ear, however innocent, hit him like a fist in the gut. He owed her his honesty, but once she knew all the details of his failed marriage, she could very well rethink accepting his proposal. Not telling her the whole truth wasn't an option. At some point he'd have to sit down with Pearl, reveal his selfish past, and leave the outcome up to God. He returned to sit at the table and finish his coffee.

"Perhaps you're right, my dear. If the weather cooperates, maybe we could take a stroll down by the creek this Sunday afternoon. It will give us time to talk."

"That sounds lovely." She bent and pulled a pan of fat biscuits from the oven.

Hubert cleared his throat and steered the conversation in a different direction. "Last night wasn't all hopeless. Everett said he realized that he loves me."

Her eyes brightened along with her beaming smile. "Well, that's certainly something to praise God for."

"Indeed." Remembering Everett's words filled him with swirling emotions. Although gratifying to hear, they were followed by Everett's insistent objection to Hubert's engagement. No use troubling Pearl with that revelation.

"Will Everett be joining us Sunday for church?"

"I haven't mentioned it yet." Hubert turned in his chair, the recollection of a smidgen of conversation with Everett tapping him on the shoulder. "He said something a few days ago about a minister back in Baltimore who came to visit his grandfather. Apparently this man spent some time talking with Everett as well. I didn't have the opportunity to ask him about it at any length, but I intend to."

He imagined the three of them sitting in service together. What would Everett think of the little Willow Creek community church? Wood floors instead of marble, no cushions on the pews, no fancy stained-glass windows, not even enough hymnbooks to go around. But the Spirit of God was evident in the way the believers worshipped, and Pastor Witherspoon preached God's Word with fervor. Hubert prayed Everett might attend with an open mind and heart.

He drained the last swallow of coffee and stood. "I'd best be going or folks will think I've taken the day off."

Pearl reached into the pantry and handed him a plate covered with a blue-checked napkin. "I wrapped up a piece of pie for you. You can have it at lunchtime."

He grinned and leaned to brush a quick kiss on her cheek. "I love you, Pearl Dunnigan, and not just for your apple pie."

She shook her head. "How can a girl resist a line like that?"

&

Pearl hummed as she ran her dust cloth over the mantel in the parlor. Since today was Saturday, it was doubtful she'd see Hubert unless she went to the mercantile. Many farm folks came into town on Saturdays, and he would be busy the entire day, but she looked forward to spending a leisurely afternoon with him tomorrow.

She moved from the parlor to her bedroom and dusted the dresser and washstand. When she came to the bedside table, she paused to pick up the silver music box and rub it until its brilliance resembled a mirror. Taking a moment, she turned the key on the side and opened the lid. Strains of Strauss's "Love Serenade" caressed her very soul, and she swayed gently back and forth, a soft smile of remembrance tickling her heart. She closed her eyes and invited the sweet memory to accompany her again.

"Yes, Hubert. I would be honored to marry you," she whispered.

A loud rapping on the front door intruded into her woolgathering.

"I'm coming," she called out, scurrying down the short hallway to the foyer. When she opened the door, she blinked in surprise.

"Everett." She stopped herself before blurting out "What are you doing here?" But the question stood front and center in her mind. "Please come in." She stepped aside to allow the young man to enter.

"Mrs. Dunnigan." He handed her his hat. "Since my father is quite busy today, I thought we might take this time to talk."

"Why of course." She hung the hat on the hall tree and gestured toward the parlor. A rueful pinch in her stomach told her Everett wouldn't appreciate being invited to sit in the kitchen for a cup of coffee. "Please sit down. May I fix you some tea?"

"No thank you." He sat in the maroon wingback chair closest to the door. Pearl speculated that he looked as if he wanted an unobstructed exit in the event he felt the need to escape. But an awareness pressed in on her that perhaps she might be the one wishing to escape by the end of this conversation. She schooled her expression and pasted on a warm smile.

"I'm so glad you stopped by. I've been hoping we could

have an opportunity to get to know each other better." The last time the young man graced her with his presence wasn't the happiest of memories. Hopefully they could start out fresh this afternoon.

"I, too, have desired the chance to talk to you." Everett propped his elbows on the arms of the chair and interlaced his fingers. "There are some things I'd like to clarify, and I feel the only way to do that is to meet the issues head-on."

Pearl nodded and took a seat across from him. The thought winged through her mind that she was glad she'd just finished cleaning this room. "I like straightforwardness as well. There's nothing to be gained by beating around the bush."

Everett raised one eyebrow in a speculative arch. "That's an interesting choice of words, Mrs. Dunnigan, because I've been wondering the same thing."

His meaning was lost on Pearl. "What is it that has you wondering?"

He sent her a skeptical look as if he doubted the validity of her question. "I don't presume to know the depth of your motives, but I can surmise."

He glanced about the room, and for the first time, Pearl felt embarrassed by the simple furnishings. But that was silly. Why should she be ashamed of the blessings God had given her? She shook off the thought and directed her mind to focus on Everett's puzzling statement.

"I'm sorry, Everett. Since we've agreed to speak plainly, perhaps you should come to the point and state the purpose for your visit."

Everett pressed his fingertips together and looked straight at her without blinking. "I am wondering about your motives, Mrs. Dunnigan. What exactly do you hope to gain by marrying my father?"

The question stole Pearl's breath. Was he implying what

she thought he was implying? "Gain?" She paused to regulate her breathing. "I hope to gain a husband who loves me as much as I love him."

A sardonic twitch lifted the corner of his mouth. "Mrs. Dunnigan, let's not pretend we don't understand each other. I'm sure you're tired of working so hard here." He waved his open hand in a sweeping gesture of the room. "My father was well paid by the Pinkerton National Detective Agency, which included a substantial retirement bonus." He leaned his head slightly forward. "Of course, you already knew that. Why else would you pursue a man whose class is far above your own?"

Pearl couldn't have been more shocked if Everett had slapped her. "Wh–what?" A tremor jolted through her and nausea stirred in her stomach. "What are you saying?"

Everett sat back in the chair, his chin raised, eyes narrowed. "I think you want to marry my father so you can live a life of ease. Marrying a man of substance would elevate your position in the community and afford you comforts you don't currently enjoy."

She sat, dumbstruck and paralyzed. Her mouth moved but nothing came out. The words stuck in her throat along with her breath. Even the muscles required to shake her head refused to work.

"Not that I blame you, you understand." His condescending tone poured buckets of humiliation over her. "Running a boardinghouse must be drudgery. You certainly wouldn't be the first woman who tried to improve her situation by marrying into money." He lifted his gaze, as though a list of offending women was written in the air. "Those gold-digging creatures who prey upon wealthy, lonely men are rather pathetic in their own conniving way."

Pearl's protest froze within her. How was she to respond to such outrageous charges? Would Everett even allow her a defense? Did he truly believe she didn't love Hubert, but rather sought to marry him for whatever material benefits might come her way? Before words could form logically in her mind, Everett rose.

"I would ask that you ponder the ramifications of your intentions. You understand, of course, that if you go through with the marriage, you will effectively drive a wedge between me and my father. Now that you know I am aware of your purpose, perhaps you'll rethink your unseemly plan." He stepped into the hallway and retrieved his hat. "Good afternoon, Mrs. Dunnigan."

Long after the door closed behind him, Pearl sat unmoving on the settee, the words she couldn't speak locked in her heart.

❧

Pearl clasped her hands in her lap trying to keep them from trembling. During the hymn singing, she'd moved her lips in a vain attempt to add her voice to the worship, but no music rang in her heart and the ache in her throat hindered words from escaping. Her Bible now lay open in her lap, but the numbness in her mind prevented comprehension of the minister's words when he announced his text. She could feel Hubert's disconcertment as he sat next to her on the pew. She dared not look at him. One glance at his tender gray eyes would be her undoing, and she must not turn back now. The pressure in her chest built with every passing minute.

Everett's presence on the other side of his father had an unsettling effect as well, and it sent shards of guilt through her. She should rejoice that Hubert's son came to church with them, but his close proximity only caused her sore heart more torment.

She hadn't closed her eyes all night, except in prayer. By dawn, she still had no peace about her decision, no clear leading from God, but she had no other choice. She knew what she had to do, and that knowledge was eating a hole through her from the inside.

People stood and moved about, and Pearl realized the service was over. She'd not heard a word of the sermon. Hubert's hand touched hers and she startled, pulling back like she'd been stung by a bee.

"Pearl, are you all right? You've been acting rather peculiar this morning." Hubert put a hand on her back and gently guided her ahead of Everett toward the door.

The trio stepped out the front door of the church and shook hands with the pastor. Since the summer day was clear and relatively mild for mid-July, Hubert had suggested they walk to church instead of riding in the buggy. The boardinghouse was a mere two blocks away, but Pearl felt as if she were walking to the gallows.

When they arrived at her gate, Everett remained by the street. She could feel his cold eyes on her while Hubert walked her to the door. It was now or never. She still couldn't bear to look directly at him, so she studied the tips of her shoes peeking out from beneath the hem of her dress. She took a deep breath. It hurt.

"Hubert, I can't go walking with you this afternoon."

"I knew something was wrong. Are you not feeling well?" Concern resonated in his voice.

"I'm fine," she lied. "Hubert, I. . .I've changed my mind. I don't think the marriage is a good idea. We simply aren't suited to each other."

Several moments of silence ticked by. Finally Hubert reached to grasp her hand, but she folded them tightly together and tucked them close to her waist.

"Pearl, what's this about? Are you nervous about the wedding? I'm told it's not uncommon for a bride to feel uneasy. Perhaps you can talk with Tessa and she can—"

"I'm not nervous about the wedding."

"What can I do to—"

"There isn't going to be a wedding." Her throat constricted and she couldn't swallow.

Hubert took hold of her upper arms. "Pearl, what's wrong? Why are you doing this?" A level of panic she'd never heard in Hubert's voice before threaded his words. "There is nothing we can't talk over, nothing we can't pray about together."

His plea for prayer almost did her in. She'd prayed—all night she'd begged God to tell her what to do. But His sovereign voice remained silent. She took a step backward away from Hubert's reach and dared to raise her eyes as far as his beard. "Hubert, please try to understand, and don't make this any more difficult than it already is. I cannot go through with this. I'm sorry." Her throat closed the rest of the way, cutting off her words as well as her air. She snatched the doorknob and pushed it, slipping inside and hastily closing the door before Hubert could say anything else.

She was surprised to feel her heart hammering against her rib cage. She'd expected it to stop altogether.

❧

As soon as she set Sunday dinner on the table for her boarders, she mumbled an excuse and slipped into her bedroom. How she wished she could latch the door and never emerge from this room again. If she did that, however, she'd lock herself in with nothing but her heartache for a companion. It was all she had.

She sank down on the bed. Her eyes instinctively moved to the silver music box on the bedside table. Picking up the treasure, she set it in her lap and raised the lid. The once angelic music now sounded like striated dissonance, haranguing against the shattered pieces of her heart. The tinkling notes mocked her. They'd become a requiem, harsh accompaniment for her own words. *You mustn't allow anything to stand in the way of reconciling with your son.* She closed the lid and warm tears dripped onto the polished silver.

# eight

Pearl hung her damp dish towel on the wooden rod beside the stove and looked around the spotless kitchen. Her aching arms and shoulders and raw knees testified to the hours she'd spent scrubbing the place for the past several days. There wasn't a square inch of floor that hadn't seen her scrub brush or a window that didn't sparkle. Every curtain had been washed, starched, and ironed, every rug hung out and beaten. Scouring the baseboards wasn't her favorite activity, but being on her knees lent itself to communing with the Father, and her boarders couldn't tell if she was wiping away sweat or tears. But keeping her hands occupied didn't quell her pining for Hubert, nor did the activity so wear her out that she didn't see his face in her dreams at night.

A knock sounded at the door, setting Pearl's senses on alert. Hubert had already come by three times trying to persuade her to talk. Her heart was too shredded to endure another encounter with him. The knock sounded again.

With one finger, she moved the curtain on the parlor window just enough to see the person standing at the front door. A gentleman stood with his back to her. He appeared to be examining the front porch. Even though she couldn't see his face, she could tell by his stature that he wasn't Hubert.

She opened the door and the man turned around. When he grinned and swept his hat from his head, she sucked in a sharp breath. His auburn hair was a little thinner than she remembered and was now peppered with streaks of gray, but the green eyes were the same.

"Pearl Dunnigan, you are a sight for sore eyes." He took a step toward her, and for a moment she thought he was going to take her in his arms.

She stepped backward, and he must have interpreted the movement as an invitation to enter. He picked up a carpetbag and crossed the threshold. Proper manners dictated that she greet him. "Mercy sakes! M–Mr. Cain, I'm surprised to see you."

He released a merry laugh. "Mr. Cain? That's rather formal, isn't it, Pearl?" He set his bag down and reached toward her. "It's good to see you, Pearl. Been way too long."

She sidestepped away from his reach. The sound of his chuckle brought back memories, and she suppressed a grimace.

She allowed a small smile. "It's. . .nice to see you, too. . . Silas. Please come in and sit down."

Silas sat in the same chair Everett occupied over a week ago. He looked around the room. "The old place hasn't changed much. Of course, neither has the town. After spending the last seven years in St. Louis and Chicago, Willow Creek is a nice break from all the noise."

Pearl flipped back the pages of her memory to the last time she'd seen Silas Cain, recalling the less than pleasant circumstances. She couldn't help wondering what he was doing here. Alone.

"How is your wife, Silas? Rebecca, wasn't that her name?"

A ripple of stiffness squirmed through him, and the smile on his face turned wooden. "Now Pearl, I tried to tell you seven years ago that was all a misunderstanding. Rebecca and I were never married. She—how shall I put this charitably? She was anxious to find a man to marry, due to her. . .um, delicate condition."

Heat flushed into Pearl's face at his words and her eyebrows rose. "That's not what she told me."

Silas uncrossed and recrossed his legs. "Of course she wouldn't admit something like that to a respectable lady like you." He shook his head, an expression of pity filling his face. "I actually felt sorry for her despite her fabrications. That's why I had given her some money when I first met her in Dubuque. She was in trouble and I wanted to help her. After all, I'm old enough to be her father. I never dreamed she would follow me, claiming to be my wife." He shook his head again. "Quite sad, really."

Since there was no way to confirm or deny Silas's explanation, Pearl couldn't very well argue, and she quite honestly didn't care. Even though Silas had tried to court her seven years ago, going so far as asking her to marry him, Pearl had no inclination to entertain him as a suitor then or now.

As if reading her thoughts, Silas's expression turned solemn. "You know you broke my heart, don't you, Pearl? After you turned down my marriage proposal, I wasn't certain what to do. I just knew I couldn't stay on here and see you every day, knowing you didn't return my love. So I tried to move ahead with my life." He sighed. "For the past seven years, I've been working with an investment firm out of St. Louis. I've done rather well, if I do say so myself."

Pearl had no desire to discuss the past with him. His dramatic explanation of the reason he'd left town almost made her roll her eyes.

Another question posed itself. "So what are you doing here, Silas? Surely cities like St. Louis and Chicago have much more to offer than our little town."

Silas cleared his throat. "Yes, well, it so happens I was glancing through the *Chicago Daily Tribune* last week and came across this." He pulled a scrap of paper from his suit pocket and held it out to her.

She took it and the words on the torn-out newspaper ad sent another slice of pain through her. *For sale—well-*

*established business in Willow Creek, Iowa. Seven-room, fully furnished boardinghouse. Contact P. Dunnigan in care of Willow Creek post office.* She swallowed hard and handed it back to him.

"When I read it, I knew it was your place. After all, how many boardinghouses are there in Willow Creek?" He chuckled like his reference to the town was a joke. "This is just the type of investment that interests my business associates." Silas tucked the scrap into his pocket and took another sweeping assessment of the room. "Could use a bit of fixing up, but if the price is right, I'm sure we can do business."

Pearl ordered the lump in her throat back down where it belonged. "I'm sorry you came all this way for nothing, Silas. The place is no longer for sale."

Disappointment flickered across his face. "You've already sold it?"

The muscles in her neck tightened with her effort to show no emotion. "No, I've decided not to sell." She fixed her eyes on the newly laundered curtains.

Silas harrumphed. "Well, I can be pretty convincing. Perhaps I can change your mind."

"No, I don't believe you can, Silas." She raised her chin and straightened her shoulders.

He sat forward. "You do still run this place as a boarding-house, don't you?"

Her aching hands and sore knees affirmed his inquiry. "Yes."

He grinned. "Well, I hope you have a vacancy because I'd like to rent a room."

The truth was she had three rooms available and renting one of them would certainly help with her finances. There were a number of things that needed to be fixed or replaced, and having one more boarder might enable her to pay for those repairs. But a warning sounded in her head. She wasn't sure having Silas Cain under her roof again was a good idea. What would the town gossipers say when they found out Silas Cain was back in town? She shook off the thought. She was in the business of renting rooms and Silas was offering to rent one.

Something didn't make sense. "If you are doing so well with this investment company, why aren't you staying in the hotel? The rooms there are much nicer than mine."

He raised one finger in the air to make his point. "Ah, but the hotel is lacking in one very special area." His eyes took on a mischievous look. "They don't have Pearl Dunnigan. So—" He rubbed his hands together. "Do you have a room available?"

She still hesitated, wishing she could tell him no. But the need to rent the room was greater than her desire to send him away. "Yes, I do have a room." No sense in admitting to him she had three empty rooms. If he thought she was desperate, he might use that to his advantage. "It's not my best room, and it's rather small. There's only one window and it has a northern exposure, and the bed is—"

Silas's booming laugh interrupted her litany. "Pearl, my dear, you are the world's worst businesswoman. You're supposed to tell me how nice the room is so I'll have to pay a higher rent, not tell me everything that's wrong with it."

*My dear.* She wished he had used any other term but that one. The only man she wished to call her *dear* was Hubert. Another painful dart stabbed her, but she stood and pulled in a breath. "The room is upstairs, the last door on the left. May I assume you will be taking breakfast and supper here as well?"

Silas stood and picked up his bag. "You may. If your cooking is still as good as I remember, that's another reason for staying here instead of the hotel." He pulled out his wallet, extracted several bills, and handed them to her. "Will that cover the first week, plus meals?"

Pearl's eyes widened as she looked at the money in her hand. "This will cover three weeks, Silas. You know my rates aren't this high."

He grinned and started toward the stairs. "Consider me paid up for three weeks."

She watched as her newest boarder climbed the stairs and turned the corner. Silas Cain—she'd all but forgotten he ever existed. Had she just made a mistake?

❧

Hubert glanced out the storefront window, looking for a wagon or some other conveyance that might belong to his customer. The rather sizable pile of goods and clothing stacked on the counter would make an unwieldy load were the gentleman to carry it.

Before Hubert could ask, the man set a pair of boots on the counter beside the other items. "Add these as well."

"Yes sir." Hubert jotted down the price of the boots. "Are you going to be settling into our community?"

The gentleman glanced up. "Why do you ask?"

Hubert studied his customer with quiet perception. "You're obviously a chap from the city. Looks like you're outfitting yourself to accommodate our more rural way of life."

The man gave a curt nod. "I didn't have time to pack much before I left Chicago. Do you deliver?"

"Yes sir. I can deliver these things this afternoon as long as it's in town." He added up the grand total. "That all comes to fourteen dollars and twenty cents, Mr. . . . ."

"Cain. Silas Cain." Mr. Cain counted out the money and laid it on the counter. "Can you deliver it to Pearl Dunnigan's boardinghouse?"

Hubert almost choked on his own breath. "Uh, yes. I can. . . have it delivered there."

"You know where the boardinghouse is?" Mr. Cain pointed down the street.

"Yes sir, I know where it is." Hearing Pearl's name caused his stomach to roll and pitch like waves on the ocean. "I'll see to it right away."

Mr. Cain bid him good day and left just as Hubert's friend Gideon Maxwell came in.

"Good morning, Gideon."

Gideon glanced over his shoulder at the departing customer. "That guy looks familiar. . . . Cain, isn't it?"

Hubert came out from behind the counter and nodded. "Yes. He said his name is Silas Cain. Do you know him?"

Gideon nudged his hat back and scratched the top of his head before tugging the hat back into place. "I sorta know him. He lived here for a short while several years back. I was only in my teens, but I remember. . ." He paused, his finger tapping his chin, and then turned back to Hubert. "It was back when my father still owned the mercantile. I remember Cain coming in the store from time to time. He stayed at Miss Pearl's place, and as I recall, he was pretty sweet on Miss Pearl."

Hubert's insides jerked into a knot. He shot a glance in the direction Cain had taken, but the man was out of sight. Had Pearl taken up with an old beau?

"Look, Hubert. . ." Gideon shuffled a booted foot. "Tessa told me what happened between you and Miss Pearl. I'm really sorry. I wish there was something we could do to change her mind."

Hubert shook his head and walked back behind the counter. "She won't talk to me. I've tried to see her, but she told me not to come back. All she said was she thought the marriage wasn't a good idea and we weren't right for each other." He pounded a fist on the counter in a rare display of frustration. "Did you ever hear such nonsense? Not right for each other. There isn't a woman on the face of the earth who is more right for me than Pearl Dunnigan." He took a slow, steadying breath. "She won't give me a real explanation."

Gideon stuffed his hands in his pockets. "Tessa told me that Miss Pearl wouldn't talk about it—just kept saying it was something she had to do. Is there any way I can help?"

Hubert gave a huff and tipped his head at the stack of goods still sitting on the counter. "There is. Can you deliver these things to Mr. Cain at the boardinghouse when I get them wrapped up?"

Gideon frowned at the items and then glanced out the door again. "This is Cain's stuff? He's staying at the boardinghouse?"

Hubert pulled out a length of store paper and began wrapping the pants and shirts. "That's what he said."

Gideon gave a low whistle. "Yeah, I'll take them by there. I have to stop at the Feed and Seed, but I'll come back here in about a half hour." He started toward the door. "Oh!" He stopped and pulled a piece of paper from his vest pocket. "Here's Tessa's list. She'd be mighty put out if I came home without these things." He handed the list to Hubert. "Don't bother wrapping any of it. I have a couple of empty crates in the back of the wagon."

Just as he reached the door, Gideon stopped again. "You know, I seem to remember. . ."

Hubert looked up from pulling a length of string around the package. "Yes?"

Gideon put his hands on his hips. "Now I remember why Silas Cain left town all those years ago." He walked back to the counter. "Cain had asked Miss Pearl to marry him. It was all over town."

The string slipped from Hubert's fingers and fell to the floor. "Are you sure?"

Gideon frowned as if pulling the recollection from the

back of his brain. "Yeah, I think I was sixteen or seventeen at the time. My dad was running the mercantile, and I helped out in here. Cain had run up a bill." Gideon rubbed his forehead as though the motion might free up the long-buried memory. He yanked his head up. "I remember now. Cain had charged a lot of stuff, and every time he came in, he told my father he was expecting a bank draft any day. His bill was almost forty dollars, as I recall. He asked Miss Pearl to marry him, and then he left town without ever paying his bill. If you look through the old record books, you'll find it. It was at least six or seven years ago."

Hubert's hands hung motionless at his sides. "He asked Pearl to marry him?" He stared at the string lying on the floor. "Why didn't he marry her?" He pulled his gaze up to meet Gideon's wry, sympathetic smile.

"She turned him down."

As he left, Gideon called back over his shoulder that he'd be back after a while to pick up his own supplies as well as Cain's, but Hubert barely heard him. Was Cain the reason Pearl broke their engagement? Hubert couldn't remember seeing Cain in town until today, but that didn't mean he hadn't been corresponding with Pearl. She could have known Cain was coming back to town.

Hubert shook his head. For that scenario to have any validity, Pearl would have to be deceptive, and the very word didn't even fit her pinkie finger. Nevertheless, her former suitor was residing under her roof again. An unfamiliar tightness growled in his chest when he wondered if Pearl's head had been turned. An acid taste filled his mouth.

Gideon's recollection of Cain running up an unpaid bill set Hubert's detective instincts in motion. The man had paid for the merchandise he purchased today, but if he had a history of not paying his bills, it was possible he might try to swindle Pearl out of the rent money. Despite the broken engagement,

Hubert couldn't stand by and watch anyone take advantage of Pearl. He'd have to devise a way to find out if he'd paid Pearl for his room. Easier said than done since she wouldn't talk to him. Perhaps Tessa could ask some discreet questions.

By the time he finished wrapping Cain's purchases, Hubert's resentment of the man nearly strangled him. Every part of him wanted to confront Cain and run him out of town. But prior experience taught him to remain calm, even friendly, around the man, if he wanted to discover Cain's intentions. And if those intentions harmed Pearl in any way, Hubert meant to see the man stopped.

He hung the BACK IN TEN MINUTES sign on the front door and locked it behind him on his way out. He strode down the street to the building that served as both the telegraph office and the stage depot.

The gray-headed telegrapher greeted him. "Howdy, Hubert. Nice day, ain't it?"

Truthfully, Hubert hadn't noticed what kind of day it was. His heart was crushed and now this interloper had returned to Willow Creek to—he wasn't certain yet what Cain's purpose was, but he intended to find out.

"Sam, I need to send a telegram." He took the pencil and paper Sam handed him and began to write.

TO ZACK PETERSON, PINKERTON NATIONAL DETECTIVE AGENCY, CHICAGO. NEED INFORMATION. *Stop.* PRIOR RECORD AND ARREST WARRANTS FOR SILAS CAIN. *Stop.* ANY INFORMATION HELPFUL. *Stop.* LETTER TO FOLLOW. *Stop.* HUBERT BEHR.

Hubert pushed the paper across the desk along with a few coins to pay for the telegram, adding an extra silver dollar. "Confidential, Sam."

Sam showed a gap-toothed smile. "You betcha."

## nine

Pearl studied the back of Hubert's head from her vantage point four rows back. She'd tried to focus her attention on Pastor Witherspoon's sermon, but the distraction of having Hubert in front of her was too great. Perhaps next Sunday she should sit on the front row.

Everett sat beside his father, his back as straight as a board. Pearl battled feelings of resentment toward the young man. *If it weren't for Everett. . .* No, she'd not think that way. Everett's presence brought joy to Hubert. Wasn't that the whole point of her stepping aside, so she wouldn't hinder the strengthening bond between them? Once more she prayed that God would remove the seeds of animosity from her heart. She'd had a choice. She could have kept Hubert selfishly to herself and watched his heart break when Everett severed relations with him. But she loved Hubert too much to come between him and his son, or to ask him to choose between them.

The pastor closed his Bible and exhorted the congregation to seek the Lord in their everyday lives, quoting from the book of Acts. "In Him we live, and move, and have our being." A few announcements followed, but Pearl paid little attention. Her mind was fixed on slipping out before Hubert could catch up to her.

As soon as the "amen" to the final prayer was spoken, Pearl stepped from her seat and hurried toward the door. Her plan fell apart, however, when Pastor Witherspoon stopped her as she shook his hand.

"Miss Pearl, I was very sorry to hear that I won't be

performing your wedding ceremony after all." His white eyebrows puckered in dismay, and he lowered his voice. "If there is anything I can do to help you and Hubert resolve your differences, please call on me. Sometimes issues arise, and they seem much larger than they really are. Often a third party, a mediator of sorts, can help a couple to see those issues from the other's viewpoint."

She heard Hubert's voice directly behind her. "You go ahead, son. I won't be long."

Pastor Witherspoon still held her hand, and it would be rude to jerk it away. The kindly minister smiled. "Prayerful consideration is always the best resolution to these disagreements. There's nothing that can't be worked out when God is in the midst." He patted her hand before releasing it.

She forced a tight smile and hurried to put distance between herself and Hubert, but in her haste she set her foot down on the edge of the step and pitched forward. When she thrust her hand out to seize the railing, her arm was captured in a strong, steadying grasp.

"Pearl, are you all right?" Hubert's voice, deep and husky, sounded next to her ear.

His grip on her arm and hand on her back felt like a safe sanctuary, but it was a place she couldn't stay, safe or not. She reluctantly pulled her arm free and smoothed her skirt, but the sensation of Hubert's touch lingered. Desiring to memorize the moment his hand came in contact with her, she slid her eyes closed for a split second.

"I'm fine, thank you." Her mumbled reply was so soft she barely heard it herself. Dare she raise her eyes to meet his? If she looked into his face at such a cozy juxtaposition, her resolve might crumble into dust. Before she could discipline her traitorous gaze, her chin tipped upward, and Hubert's dear image came into view.

Heat rose from her midsection to flood her face. His eyes spoke what his lips didn't, and she could not remain in his proximity.

"Excuse me. . ."

"Pearl, might we speak privately?"

She halted. Other people were emerging from the church, and she had no wish to be on display or become a topic of tomorrow's gossip. Praying for steel in her spine, she turned halfway. Hubert stepped beside her.

"Please, Pearl—"

"I'm sorry, Hubert." She restrained her feet from running but held her pace to a ladylike walk, grateful that she didn't hear Hubert's footsteps following her. Watching carefully where she placed her feet, she nearly collided with a man standing at the far edge of the churchyard.

"Oh!" She jerked her gaze up and encountered Everett, watching her. His cynical expression chilled her.

"Are you quite all right, Mrs. Dunnigan?" She didn't miss the acerbity in his tone.

"Yes, thank you." She sent him a polite nod, and he touched the brim of his hat in return.

Never before had the desire to get home driven her with such urgency. She walked briskly along the boardwalk, trying to forget the events from the churchyard. Despite the initial desire to indelibly etch Hubert's touch into her memory, now she thought better of it. No good would come of filling her mind and thoughts with longings she could never realize.

She turned the corner and caught sight of Silas walking toward her. The same wariness that caused her to hesitate about renting him a room filled her again.

"Good morning, Pearl. Isn't it a lovely day?"

"I thought you had a headache. Isn't that why you said you couldn't attend church?"

Silas fell into step beside her. "Ah, the cup of tea you gave me must have been a magical elixir because the headache melted away."

Pearl cut her gaze sideways to take in his profile. "I'm glad it helped. Dinner will be ready soon."

They came to the white picket gate that led to the boardinghouse porch, and Silas held it open for her in gallant fashion. "You know, it's too bad you have to hurry home to so many duties. I should think you'd hire a cook and a maid to perform the chores for you."

Pearl stopped on the porch steps and turned to aim an incredulous stare his way. "Hire a cook and a maid? Mercy sakes, I'd have to double everyone's rent to afford that. Besides, you said my cooking was the reason you preferred to stay here instead of the hotel." She continued across the porch and Silas hastened to hold the door open.

"One of the reasons, Pearl."

She chose not to explore further possibilities but rather hurried to the kitchen. Silas followed her and leaned against the worktable.

"You know, I have a very promising enterprise in the planning stages."

Pearl tied her apron on and flicked a glance his way. Why he thought she would be interested in his business deals, she had no idea, but she wished he'd leave her kitchen.

"If things work out the way I foresee, I'll be in a very good position." He inspected his fingernails and buffed them on his lapel. "I could help you in a lot of ways, Pearl."

She waggled her fingers in a gesture for him to move out of her way so she could mix the biscuit dough. "What makes you think I need help?"

He moved around the opposite side of the table and faced her. "Pearl, look at how hard you work. If you'll allow me, I could make it so you'll never have to work like this again."

Pearl's hands halted mid-motion. Whatever in the world

was he talking about? "Silas, I'm sure you mean well, but I don't need any help. Now if you'll excuse me, I need to get these biscuits in the oven."

"Perhaps later, when you aren't so. . .distracted, we can talk in more detail." Silas excused himself and left the room.

Pearl continued scurrying about the kitchen, but she couldn't help wondering what initiated Silas's speculation. Once more, she questioned her decision to rent him a room.

❧

Pearl sat alone on an old quilt between two cedars in a corner of the churchyard. Silas decided at the last minute to accompany Pearl to church and attend the picnic afterward, but he'd struck up a conversation with one of the local businessmen, leaving Pearl to herself. Taking advantage of her solitude and the privacy afforded by the cedar boughs, Pearl had a clear view of Hubert spreading his blanket under the cedars across the yard. She knew she shouldn't allow her musings to include Hubert, but her thoughts often took on a will of their own, and like it or not, he remained first and foremost in her dreams—both night and day.

Had circumstances been different, she and Hubert might be married by now and sharing the shady spot. Now she wished she'd told Tessa no when her friend had urged her to come to the church picnic.

"Mind if we share this quiet spot with you, Grandma Pearl?" Tessa slipped down onto Pearl's quilt, holding a very cranky toddler by the hand. "I think she might nap if she's away from all the activity."

Pearl smiled and pulled Susan into a hug. "Just the company I needed." She laid the child in the middle of the quilt and gently rubbed her back until Susan's eyes closed.

"I thought you looked a little lonely." Tessa gave Pearl an understanding smile. "After all the coaxing I had to do, I'm surprised you came by yourself."

A sigh escaped, but Pearl didn't try to hold it in. The longing in her heart heightened when she looked across the yard at Hubert, sitting alone and picking at the food on his plate.

Tessa reached across the quilt and squeezed Pearl's shoulder. "Why don't you go talk to him and clear up whatever it is that has come between you. Look at the two of you. You're both miserable."

Pearl slipped her hand up to cover Tessa's. "I appreciate your concern, honey, really I do. But it's not that simple. Besides, I didn't come by myself."

Tessa's eyes widened. "You didn't? Who did you come with?"

Not wanting Tessa to get the wrong idea, Pearl flapped her hand and shook her head. "It's not what you think. One of my boarders decided to come to church today, and when I told him there was going to be a picnic afterward, he asked if he could accompany me. That's all."

Tessa leaned forward. "Is it that new man, Mr. Cain?"

Now it was Pearl's turn for surprise. "How did you know that?"

Tessa shrugged. "I suppose I heard someone talking about it."

Pearl groaned. "Who was talking? What were they saying?"

A sheepish grimace stretched across Tessa's face, and she lifted her shoulders. "Gideon said Mr. Cain used to live here a few years ago. Then he heard a man in the post office the other day saying Mr. Cain was back in town and he was probably here to see you." She tipped her head close to Pearl's shoulder and lowered her voice. "Two ladies in the butcher shop yesterday said Mr. Cain proposed to you a few years ago." Tessa's gaze shifted left and right. "Is that true? Did Mr. Cain ask you to marry him?"

Pearl covered her eyes with her hand and shook her head in trepidation. "Yes, it's true. Mr. Cain tried to court me, but that was seven years ago. I suppose rumors are flying all over town."

Tessa leaned back and brushed a lock of downy hair from her sleeping child's face. "I don't know about all over town. I think people are just curious. Most folks know you and Hubert were engaged."

Pearl let out a huff. "Silas Cain is one of my boarders. Nothing more." She stretched her arms, then propped them behind her, leaning back slightly and taking in a slow, deep breath. "I can't change what folks want to believe."

She let her gaze wander across the yard again. Hubert was no longer sitting on the blanket by the cedars, but Everett was there with a young lady. Pearl squinted her eyes and put a hand up to shade them against the sun's glare. Everett's companion appeared to be Tillie O'Dell, a girl Tessa had worked with at the hotel a couple of years back.

"Is that Tillie sitting with Everett?"

Tessa craned her neck. "I believe it is. Tillie is such a sweet girl."

While Tessa continued to chatter, Pearl sent a searching sweep across the expanse of the wide yard. Hubert was nowhere in sight, but Silas was heading in her direction, apparently to claim her attention for the remainder of the afternoon. The day's end couldn't come soon enough as far as Pearl was concerned.

❧

The tension in Pearl's neck and shoulders had crept up into the back of her head, and all she wished to do was disengage herself from Silas's company. After enduring the walk back to the boardinghouse, listening to his prattle about his successful business ventures, she finally excused herself and closed her bedroom door. She slipped into her nightgown and folded the bedcovers back. Lowering herself slowly to her knees, she leaned forward on the bed and clasped her hands. "Dear Lord, it's been quite a day. I don't have to tell You about this pain in my heart that won't leave me alone. But I don't know how to make it stop other than asking You to take it away.

"Lord, folks are talking, as folks are prone to do, but I'm not used to being the topic of conversation. It doesn't seem like there's anything I can do about that either, so I'll leave the gossipers to You.

"I'm not sure what to make of Silas being here. He says he has business here, and I'm asking You to help him finish whatever his business is so he can leave." Pearl sighed and shook her head. "I don't mean to tell you what to do, Lord. I'm sure You have a plan for Silas being here. You are a God of second chances and maybe that's what You're asking me to do where Silas is concerned. But I have no feelings for Silas. Never did. How can I do that when Hubert occupies my heart?" She felt an immediate check in her spirit. Was the Lord cautioning her about Silas's intentions or allowing Hubert to remain steadfastly in her heart?

She ended her prayer and slipped into bed, but despite her weariness, sleep remained elusive. Questions still tarried on her mind and images of Hubert lingered in her very soul.

❧

"I wish you hadn't left the picnic, Father. People were asking me where you were." The look Everett sent across the room at Hubert was bereft of any real annoyance but rather edged with concern.

Hubert gazed at the ebbing flames in the fireplace and took another sip of his favorite tea. He cared little what people thought, unless the one asking was Pearl. Despite the spread of delectable treats brought by the ladies of the congregation, every bite he'd eaten was tasteless.

"I'm afraid I wasn't very good company today, and I didn't wish to spoil the fellowship." He angled a look at Everett.

"Besides, I noticed you were keeping company with Miss Tillie, and I presumed you'd rather be alone."

A slight blush crept into Everett's cheeks. "She's a delightful young woman, easy to talk to, and not flighty and giggly like some I've known. All in all, the afternoon was quite enjoyable."

Hubert nodded. "I agree she's a lovely girl." He wondered if Everett knew her father was a farmer and Tillie herself worked in the hotel dining room. "She comes from a fine Christian family."

Everett pulled his eyebrows into a thoughtful frown and set his teacup down. "I've noticed you often refer to a person being a Christian like it's something special and unique. You sound very much like the minister back in Baltimore who came to visit Grandfather."

A surge of hope filled Hubert's chest. "You must understand, son, being a Christian isn't something you inherit. You told me that you are waiting to hear from your grandfather's attorney regarding your inheritance. You also mentioned that this minister said your grandfather *knew* Jesus." He paused a moment to let Everett respond, but his son remained silent and simply nodded as though mulling over his father's words. So Hubert continued.

"You might inherit money or property from your grandfather's estate, but you cannot inherit the relationship he had with Jesus Christ. When you acknowledge the sinfulness of your heart—and all of us have sinned—and desire to accept the payment of Christ's death as atonement for that sin, you inherit eternal life. But you don't inherit it from your grandfather, you inherit it from God. You become His child. It's a decision you must make on your own."

Hubert's heart thumped in hopeful anticipation. He'd prayed for the opportunity to share his faith with Everett. Gratefulness flooded his soul, especially when Everett didn't respond with indignation as Hubert feared he might.

Everett sat quietly for several minutes staring at the dying fire. Finally he rose. "I think I understand what you're saying, Father. Reverend Werner explained it much the same way. You've given me quite a lot to think about." He started toward his bedroom but stopped and turned back to Hubert. "You say Tillie and her family believe this way also?"

Hubert clasped his fingers together. "Not being able to examine their hearts the way God can, I can't say for certain. But when a person becomes a child of God, it's usually evidenced in their life. That being the case, I think I can be relatively sure that Tillie and her family are Christians because of the testimony they live. When Jesus is in residence, a change occurs in the person's life that's hard to hide."

Everett nodded. "Hmm. Well, good night, Father."

"Good night."

After Everett's door closed, Hubert sat watching the glowing embers in the fireplace fade. He whispered a prayer of thanksgiving for Everett's willingness to listen, and once again asked God to send the power of the Holy Spirit to deal with Everett's heart. Only one thing squeezed him with regret. He wished he could share this answer to prayer with Pearl.

# ten

Pearl glanced through her mail as she exited the post office. Even the envelope with her favorite niece's return address on it failed to stir her excitement. She glanced down the street where the mercantile doors stood open. Oh how she longed to march straight inside and tell Hubert she'd marry him no matter what Everett thought, but she'd already made her choice. There was no going back.

She crossed the street and headed toward the Feed and Seed. In order to keep the residents of the boardinghouse in fresh vegetables all season, as well as have enough to can for the winter, she needed to plant more peas, carrots, cabbage, and parsnips in her garden. The tedious work hoeing the ground in preparation for the late summer and early autumn vegetables would be a welcome diversion. Anything that kept her hands busy and her mind occupied helped to head off the melancholy moods that haunted her.

"Mrs. Dunnigan."

Pearl looked up to see Everett coming toward her. She hesitated. Given their last conversation, the young man must have already fired every poison dart in his arsenal at her. She certainly hoped he wasn't planning on further accusing her of any more ulterior motives. She set her lips in a tight line and waited for him to approach.

"Mrs. Dunnigan, forgive me for interrupting your day." He glanced around. Was he afraid someone might see him speaking to her? "I wonder if you would agree to accompany me somewhere we might talk privately."

She bit her lip to keep from blurting out what she truly

wanted to say. Instead, she raised her eyes to meet his in an unblinking stare. There was little Hubert's son could say or do at this point to inflict any more pain than he'd already done.

"I can't imagine there being anything else you need to say to me, Everett. I fulfilled your wishes, only because I care so much for your father." Was it her imagination or did she see a grimace flit across Everett's features? "I will not stand in the way of you and your father growing closer. I believe I've proven that. Now if you'll excuse me. . ."

She started to step around him, but his hand on her arm stopped her in her tracks.

"Please, Mrs. Dunnigan."

The arrogance that had laced his tone three weeks ago was absent. Curious, but wary, she nodded. "All right." Common sense told her to employ caution. Like one who learned by touching a hot stove, she wouldn't be burned again. "Can't you say whatever is on your mind right here?" There weren't many people coming and going on the boardwalk in front of the Feed and Seed, but the noise of horses and wagons driving by necessitated the raising of voices.

"I stopped by the boardinghouse, but you were out." Everett glanced up at the sky and shaded his eyes. "Why don't we go someplace where we can get out of the sun? The hotel dining room, perhaps."

Pearl wasn't sure why she agreed, but she gave him a single nod and walked along beside him. Had he, by chance, had a change of heart? If he started accusing her again of improprieties, she would simply walk away and not dignify his outrageous claims with a reply.

He held the hotel door open and escorted her to the dining room. Too late for breakfast and too early for lunch, the dining room was nearly deserted. Everett led her to a table close to the entry but tucked into a nook. Three months earlier she and Hubert had sat at this very table the first evening he had taken her to dinner. Pearl swallowed back the tightness in her throat.

He held her chair before seating himself. She waited for him to speak.

"Mrs. Dunnigan, this is rather awkward, but I feel I must ask something of you."

Pearl had no intention of indicating her agreement with his request until he'd spoken his mind. "You may ask, and I may refuse, depending on what it is. But I will hear you out."

A fleeting glimpse of relief softened his eyes for a moment. He folded his hands in front of him and studied them before raising his gaze to her again. "First of all, thank you for agreeing to listen. You are under no constraint to heed anything I say."

They agreed on that much.

He cleared his throat. "I am quite concerned about my father."

Pearl's defensive posture fell away and instantly her senses were piqued. Her first instinct was to immediately see to Hubert's welfare, but she'd seen him earlier that very morning sweeping the boardwalk in front of the store, so she knew he wasn't ill. Or was he?

"What's wrong? Hubert isn't sick, is he?" She tried but couldn't modulate her voice, and concern for Hubert's health and well-being wove its way into her inquiry.

"No, at least not physically sick." Slight lines appeared between Everett's brows. "That is, not yet. These past few weeks, my father seems to have fallen into a state of depression. He doesn't eat except a bite or two. He sleeps poorly. I hear him up at night, pacing. He has dark circles under his eyes and his complexion is pale. He seems quite listless. Often his thoughts are distracted, and he is unable to carry on a conversation without asking me to repeat something I just said."

Pearl lowered her gaze to her hands. Everett had just described her own habits for the past weeks. Her heart longed to go to Hubert, but she could not. Everett's candid remarks revealed a transparent side of the young man she'd not seen before. If Everett was thinking of someone besides himself, perhaps he wasn't the self-serving individual she thought him to be. Quite frankly, she didn't understand why he was telling her these things. How did he think she could help if he'd demanded she break the engagement?

"There is talk. . ." Everett shifted his gaze aside. "Your new boarder, a Mr. Cain, if I am not mistaken, was once a suitor of yours."

Heat ignited in Pearl's middle and rose to her face. Was everyone in town gossiping about her? She clamped her teeth tightly and waited for Everett to continue.

"Mrs. Dunnigan, I don't mean to be impertinent, but I wondered if you and Mr. Cain have renewed your courtship."

*Impertinent* didn't begin to describe her opinion of his question, but she held her temper. No good would come of a display of anger, but she became aware that if pushed far enough, her self-control might give way. She took a deep breath.

"Mr. Cain expressed his wish to court me several years ago, which I refused. He is a paying customer at the boardinghouse, nothing more." She narrowed her eyes at Everett. "Not that it is any of your business. I can't help wondering why you are asking such a personal question, and what does it have to do with Hubert not eating or sleeping well?"

A flush crept up his neck. At least he had the grace to appear uncomfortable. "Mrs. Dunnigan, despite what you may think, I care very much about my father. I am distressed to see him making himself sick. I thought perhaps, if you and Mr. Cain announced your intentions, my father could free himself of any lingering thoughts of his courtship with you being revived, thus allowing him to move past his melancholy moods."

Outrage rushed into her chest and threatened to explode. How dare he make such a suggestion! Before she could express her offense, the waitress came to take their order.

"Hello, Miss Pearl."

Pearl glanced up to see Tillie O'Dell's pretty face. The girl sent Everett a shy smile and lowered her dark lashes in a demure fashion.

"Hello, Everett. It's nice to see you again."

Everett cast a puzzled glance toward Tillie. Pearl watched the scope of his gaze take in her apron and the tray in her hands.

"What may I bring you?" Tillie pulled a pad and pencil from her apron pocket.

The expression on Everett's face changed from confusion to disbelief, and then to disdain. If Pearl's vexation over his shocking and insulting suggestion wasn't so great, she might have found his disconcertment comical.

He looked away from Tillie and cleared his throat. "Tea, please. Cream and sugar. Mrs. Dunnigan?" His abruptness took Pearl aback. This certainly wasn't the attitude he'd displayed last Sunday at the church picnic. Quite the contrary, he and Tillie had seemed to enjoy each other's company. So why was he now acting like he didn't know her?

"Uh, nothing, thank you, Tillie." She looked into Tillie's face and saw bewilderment, even though the girl's focus was on Everett.

Tillie bit her lower lip for a moment. "Everett, I wanted to tell you again what a nice time I had at the picnic."

A momentary flinch raced across Everett's face, and he slid a glance around the room. "Just the tea, please."

Tillie blinked and took a backward step. If Everett's

demeaning suggestion to take up with Silas Cain incensed Pearl, his blatant condescending attitude toward Tillie magnified her anger even further. As soon as Tillie hurried away, Pearl stood and picked up her reticule. Every nerve ending in her body wanted to shout her indignation at Hubert's son, but to do so would only further alienate him. However, regardless of his treatment of her, she refused to stand by and watch a sweet girl like Tillie hurt.

She sucked in a steadying breath and rose from her chair. "Everett, I'm going to forget this meeting took place, except for one thing." Pearl lifted her chin and straightened her shoulders. "Tillie O'Dell is a lovely, sweet Christian girl, and for you to snub her the way you just did is simply. . .mean and hateful."

She didn't bother to wish him a good day as she turned and marched resolutely out the door.

❧

Hubert ran his hand over a bolt of new material he'd just pulled from the crate and placed on the shelf. Blue, Pearl's favorite color. The fabric with its tiny forget-me-not pattern sprinkled over it was the same shade as Pearl's eyes. Maybe when she came into the mercantile, he'd just give her a dress length. *If* she came in. She'd not set foot in the store in over three weeks. He suspected that she'd coaxed Tessa to pick up supplies for the boardinghouse.

He'd caught glimpses of Pearl at church or as she walked down the boardwalk. His heart wanted to call out to her, but he couldn't embarrass her that way. The day he'd caught her when she tripped on the church steps, she'd made it clear that she considered a public confrontation inappropriate. He'd considered writing a letter, but he could only imagine the postmaster's amusement when Hubert spent two cents to mail a letter he could walk down the block and deliver in person for free.

He glanced toward the door, like he did a hundred times a day, hoping to see Pearl entering. Instead, a young lad with unruly brown hair and too many freckles to count stepped through the door. With only a cursory peek at the candy jars lined up on the counter, the youth marched up to Hubert.

"Hullo, Mr. Behr. Fine day, ain't it?"

The boy's precociousness pulled Hubert's mouth into a smile. "Hello there, young fellow. I believe I've seen you at church, haven't I?"

"Yessir. I'm Grady O'Dell."

"How nice that you've come to visit, Mr. O'Dell."

A few of Grady's freckles went into hiding when the boy grinned. "I ain't here to visit. I'm workin'."

Hubert chuckled. "Is that so? Well then, how may I assist you today, sir?"

Grady dug into his pocket, the tip of his tongue stuck out in concentration. He extracted a wrinkled scrap of paper, which he held out to Hubert. "This here's the list. I'm gettin' paid a nickel to take these things to—" He clapped his hand over his mouth, eyes wide.

Hubert took the paper and ruffled the boy's hair. "Don't you worry, Grady. I won't tell anyone about your good fortune." He unfolded the paper. "Now, let's have a look at your employer's list and—"

The handwriting on the paper was as familiar as his own. *Pearl.* Realization sent a stab of remorse through him. Pearl apparently wanted to separate herself from him and was paying Grady to pick up and deliver her groceries.

"Got my cart out on the boardwalk," Grady declared. "I'm a lot stronger than I look, so I can load it myself. Oh, and I got the money right here." He pulled a wadded-up hanky from his other pocket. When he set it on the counter, coins clinked inside its folds.

Hubert rubbed his hand over his bearded chin. So that's

the way it was. His heart grappled with his common sense. Why couldn't he simply take the supplies to Pearl himself?

"Well now, there's no need for you to tote all these things." Hubert flapped Pearl's list. "I can deliver them to Miss Pearl this afternoon."

Grady's eyes bugged out. "How didja know they was for Miss Pearl? I wasn't s'posed to tell."

Hubert patted the boy's shoulder. "It doesn't matter. But I'd be more than happy to deliver these items to her personally."

Grady's bottom lip stuck out in a pout. "But then I can't earn my nickel. I was gonna buy some peppermint sticks for my sister Tillie's birthday."

Hubert bent at the waist and put his hands on his knees. "Tell you what. I'll give you the peppermint sticks. How's that?"

A frown tainted Grady's countenance and he shook his head vehemently. "Uh-uh! My pa says a man should do a day's work for a day's pay. I want to do what Miss Pearl's payin' me to do."

How was Hubert supposed to refute that? He straightened and heaved a sigh. "All right, son. It'll take me a few minutes to get everything on this list together. Why don't you go look at the peppermint sticks."

Grady's frown dissipated, and he stuck his hand out to Hubert. "Yessir."

Hubert shook the boy's hand and began making Pearl's selections. After he wrapped up each item, and while Grady was still distracted, he quickly measured out a dress length of the blue forget-me-not material and added a yard of lace trim. Discreetly folding store paper around the yard goods, he tucked the package between Pearl's other supplies.

"Here you go, Grady. Everything is ready." Hubert counted out the money from Grady's hanky while the boy loaded the packaged items into the handcart.

All smiles, Grady waved good-bye to Hubert and turned the cart toward the boardinghouse. Hubert waved back, the pain in his heart so sharp he thought it might draw blood.

How he wished he could deliver those goods into Pearl's hands himself, but he had a terrible feeling she would close the door in his face. She'd never given him a reason for breaking their engagement, and when she'd told him not to come back, he'd abided by her wishes. For the hundredth time, he questioned his judgment.

If her decision not to marry him had anything to do with Silas Cain, why was he standing by allowing it to happen? What kind of man was he that he'd let the woman he loved walk away without fighting for her? No, he couldn't go on like this any longer. Somehow he had to make her listen. He must think of a way to catch her alone so he could talk to her without Cain's interference. In the meantime, he intended to grab hold of God's throne and beg Him for favor.

## eleven

Hubert poured two cups of coffee and carried them to the table, setting one in front of Everett before returning to his own chair. Neither of them had done justice to their supper plates. Hubert's appetite had abandoned him a few weeks ago, but Everett pushed his food around on his plate, ate little, and spoke even less.

"Is everything all right, son?"

Everett jerked his head up. "I beg your pardon?"

Hubert studied his son a moment. The air of pomposity that usually accompanied Everett's tone and manner was noticeably absent, but a frown of contemplation had carved creases in his brow for the past two days.

"Care to talk about it?" Hubert sipped his coffee.

Everett pushed his plate away and leaned back in his chair. "Father, why didn't you tell me Tillie worked in the hotel dining room?"

Hubert gave a shrug. "I don't know. . .why? Is it important?"

"Important!" Everett nearly spewed the word. "She's a waitress, a servant. Do you realize how foolish I felt?" He leaned forward and jabbed his finger into the air in Hubert's direction. "Father, she stood there in her apron waiting to take our order, telling me what a good time she had at the picnic."

Hubert folded his arms across his chest. "Frankly, I don't see the problem. If you liked Tillie at the picnic, why wouldn't you like her now that you know she works at the hotel?" His deliberately calm demeanor seemed to irritate Everett further, but Hubert went on before Everett had the chance to retort. "I tried to explain to you—the people of Willow Creek are fine, hardworking folks, and they aren't judged by their wealth or lack thereof. This isn't Baltimore. Social registers mean nothing here. You aren't any better than Tillie O'Dell because you were raised in affluence and she wasn't."

Everett opened his mouth, but Hubert held up his hand. "What makes a person worthy of your respect? Position? Status? Power? If that's the case, you must not hold me in very high esteem. I'm simply a storekeeper."

"That's different," Everett countered. "You chose to be a storekeeper. You just wanted something to do when you retired."

Hubert nodded. "Yes, that's so. But nevertheless, I wear an apron and I serve the people who come into the mercantile, the same as Tillie wears an apron and served you in the hotel dining room. She is still the same person she was at the picnic."

Everett turned and stared out the window, frustration edging his expression. "My upbringing isn't something I can casually toss away."

"I'm not asking you to do any such thing." Hubert rose from his chair. "Your grandparents were fine people." He picked up his coffee mug and carried it to the sitting area, gesturing for Everett to join him. "Are you telling me your grandparents would approve of you holding someone in contempt because they didn't have as much as you?"

The hard edges of Everett's indignation softened as he sank into the overstuffed chair by the fireplace. Hubert could see him thoughtfully weighing the question.

Finally Everett answered. "Grandfather wouldn't." His fingers curled around the ends of the armrests. "Grandfather treated everyone the same regardless of their position. Grandmother was the one who insisted on observing proper social protocol." After a minute, he looked across at Hubert, a tiny smirk tweaking the corner of his mouth. "Grandmother would have been appalled at me attending a church picnic and sitting on a blanket on the ground. She would have needed her smelling salts had she known I'd spent the afternoon with a young woman who worked as a waitress."

Hubert pressed the tips of his fingers together and allowed Everett time to contemplate the difference between the values taught by his grandparents. "So is Tillie your picnic companion different from Tillie the waitress?"

Everett didn't reply immediately. He drew in a deep breath and let it out slowly, dragging his hand through his hair. "That's something I'm going to have to think about." His expression took on a faraway look, and he spoke more to himself than to Hubert. "When she came to take our order, she smiled the same way she did at the picnic."

"Our order?"

"Mrs. Dunnigan and myself."

Hubert sat forward so abruptly his coffee sloshed over the rim of his mug. "You and Pearl were at the hotel dining room together? When was this?"

Everett jolted out of his reverie. Telltale redness crept into his complexion. "Uh, a couple of days ago."

"Why didn't you mention this to me?" Every nerve ending in Hubert's body stood at attention.

Discomfort etched a frown into Everett's brow again. "I simply ran into her in town."

"You ran into Pearl in the hotel dining room?"

"Well no, not exactly." Everett shifted his position and examined his fingernails. "I invited her to have a cup of tea."

Hubert sat, stunned. Was his son having a change of heart about Pearl? He'd love to prod Everett into disclosing what they'd talked about, but his son's countenance had closed up tighter than shutters over a window before a storm.

Was a cup of tea all it took to persuade Pearl to engage in conversation?

"Perhaps I'll do the same."

Everett's quizzical look begged an explanation.

Hubert pulled himself out of his chair and stood. "I had planned to go over to the boardinghouse this evening and try to convince Pearl to talk to me. Perhaps a cup of tea will help smooth the way."

"What?" Everett stood and faced his father. "She broke off the engagement. There's no need—"

"No need to what, son?" Hubert stared at him. "You sound like you know why she broke the engagement."

The red in Everett's face deepened. "All I know is she made her choice. Why do you insist on talking to her now that her attention is elsewhere?"

Hubert nailed Everett in place with a steel gaze. "You seem to know an awful lot about this." He took a deep breath, glanced down, and released the air on a restrained sigh. "Ever since you and I began corresponding a year ago, I prayed that we could someday be reconciled. Your being here is the answer to that prayer."

Hubert crossed the room to stand in front of the window. He stared across the expanse of the hillside that separated his house from the edge of town. Just past the treetops, the peak of the boardinghouse roof pointed skyward. The lengthening shadows and the golden hues of the descending sun winked together against the wood-shingled rooftop. Under that roof resided the woman he felt God had chosen for him.

"Everett, I don't know if you had anything to do with Pearl's decision. I don't know if her new boarder, that Cain fellow, had anything to do with it. But I know this." He turned, wanting Everett to see the determination in his expression. "I will not let her go without a fight." The waning light revealed disconcertment on his son's face. "I love Pearl.

And as happy as I am that you have come to Willow Creek, I cannot let you or anyone else stand in the way of Pearl and me being together."

Everett skewed his lips into a sneer. "I can't believe this. Twenty years ago you chose your job over your family." He thrust a hand out toward Hubert. "You *say* you're glad we've reconciled. You *say* my being here is an answer to your prayers." Sarcasm threaded his tone.

Hubert took a step forward. "I *am* glad, son. You must know that. But you must also know you cannot dictate to me how to live."

Dead silence reigned for the space of a few seconds while Everett narrowed his eyes into a reproachful glare. "Where were your prayers when I was a child, Father? Did God tell you to turn your back on your family? Was the lure of adventure what kept you away for weeks and months at a time while my mother spent her days and nights in fear, wondering where you were and if you were coming back? What was I supposed to think back then? Both my parents deserted me, my father in favor of his job and my mother for another man. Where was God then? Or was ambition your god?"

The same accusations Hubert had hurled at himself repeatedly over the years now flowed unchecked from his son's lips. The bitter remorse he thought he'd finally put behind him reemerged as needle pricks to his soul. God may have forgiven him, but until he forgave himself, guilt would continue to haunt him.

But apparently Everett wasn't finished. "Now, just when you have finally begun to act like a father, you're making the same choice you made twenty years ago. Except this time it's not your job, it's a woman."

The way Everett said *woman* sounded so disparaging Hubert almost drew his fist back. Only the knowledge he deserved his son's scorn kept him from doing so. He turned back to the window. Was the acid anger in his chest aimed at Everett or himself?

"Well, Father? Isn't it true?"

Hubert waited until his breathing slowed before answering. "Everett, I admit I was wrong all those years ago. I was so enamored with my job, everything else paled in significance. I chose to take the cases that kept me on the trail for a long time. Deep inside, I knew it was wrong to leave you and your mother alone. I should have left those cases to the unmarried men. But all I focused on was solving the toughest cases so I could gain recognition and status."

He turned to look at Everett. As painful as he knew it would be, he had to look his son in the eye when the words he had to speak crossed his lips. "Don't you see? I was guilty of putting prestige at a higher level of importance than anything else, including my family. . .and God." He swallowed hard. "I allowed ambition and success to blind me. I disobeyed God. I chose to do what I wanted instead of what God was telling me."

The lump in his throat restricted his air, but he had to make Everett understand his remorse. "The day I learned your mother had left, I came face-to-face with my own sinful selfishness. I haven't lived a single day since without regret."

Moisture glinted in Everett's eyes and Hubert crossed to him, taking hold of his son's shoulders. "Everett, you're my son and I love you. It is still my deep desire for us to be close. If I had the opportunity to rethink my choices, I'd do things differently." His fingers squeezed into Everett's shoulders. A quiver passed through his son's stiffened muscles. "I'd give anything to reclaim the time I lost being your father, but I can't."

He dropped his hands. A mixture of sorrow, relief, and hope stirred within him. A surprising lightness eased the pressure in his chest, confession releasing the burden of guilt he'd carried for so long. There would always be consequences and regrets connected with his past disobedience, and he still didn't know if he'd ever feel the right to forgive himself, but one thing was certain. God's forgiveness was absolute.

"I believe God has given me a second chance to be the kind of husband He meant for me to be twenty years ago. And that's why I'm going to go talk to Pearl. If she won't listen tonight, I'll go again tomorrow, and the day after that, and the day after that, until she believes how much I love her. I only pray I'm not too late."

Everett's posture sagged, as though drained of energy to fight. "All right, Father, if that's your decision, I won't argue and I won't try to stop you." Grief darkened Everett's eyes. His voice lacked all hint of animosity or arrogance. "Tomorrow I'll inquire about stage connections to Dubuque and train schedules east. I'll be leaving at the end of the week."

Hubert's stomach muscles tightened. Saying good-bye to Everett would break his heart. He wished his son knew the power of God's forgiveness. Perhaps if he did, he'd be able to find it in his heart to extend forgiveness to his father.

❧

Pearl was up to her elbows in dishwater when she heard the knock at the back door. She frowned and glanced through the red gingham-curtained window. "It's almost dark outside. Who is stopping by at this time of the evening?"

She grabbed a dish towel and wiped her hands on the way to the door. The moment she cracked the door open, her breath caught in her throat.

"Hubert." His name came out in a hoarse whisper.

He stood before her, holding a blue and white china teapot and a box of her favorite chamomile and ginger tea. "Hello, Pearl. Please don't close the door. I just want to talk, and thought perhaps we could share a cup of tea."

Pearl couldn't find her voice. She knew she should tell him to go away, but her heart refused to allow her tongue to work. She tried to shake her head but found herself nodding instead. Why was she opening the door wider?

"Thank you." Hubert stepped across the threshold into the kitchen. "I'll even put the water on to boil and brew the tea if you'd like."

She flapped her fingers and took the box of tea from him. "The kettle is still warm from supper." She pushed it over the hottest part of the stove. "Hubert, you shouldn't be here."

"Why?" He set the china teapot on the table. "You know I still love you, Pearl. Nothing has changed for me except the fact that you've broken our engagement. And you won't even give me a good reason for doing so."

Her heart kicked against her ribs. She couldn't answer him. How could she tell him Everett was the cause? She sidestepped the issue. "Grady O'Dell made a mistake the other day when he delivered my supplies. There was a piece of yard goods that I didn't order. I'll go and get it for you."

She started to go to her bedroom to fetch the material, but Hubert's gentle hand on her elbow held her in place. "Pearl, there was no mistake. I knew it was your list. I recognized your handwriting. I know you so well, I even know how you cross your *T*s. The cloth was a gift. It matches your eyes."

The simmering kettle covered the sound of the breath that caught in her throat. Her hands shook as she measured the tea into the china pot and poured in the scalding water.

"Hubert, that was thoughtful, but I can't accept a gift from you." Immediately her mind was stricken. Hubert's silver music box sat on her nightstand. Anguish twisted her stomach when she knew she must return the music box that she loved. Perhaps it was better if she did give it back. Every time she looked at it, tears burned her eyes. When she lifted the lid and listened to the tinkling notes, the love she kept locked away in her heart begged for release.

"I want you to have it, Pearl."

She winced. How could simple words cut so deeply? Even if Hubert referred to the blue material, how she wished she felt free to keep the music box. Hubert went to the breakfront and retrieved two teacups while she stood, fighting with her emotions. If he didn't leave soon, she'd lose her resolve.

Hubert set the cups on the table and pulled out Pearl's chair and held it for her. But she didn't sit. Instead, she balled up one corner of her apron and clenched it in her fingers.

"Hubert, I can't do this. Please go."

In one stride he was beside her and grasped her trembling hands. "Why, Pearl? Just tell me why."

She shook her head and closed her eyes. "It's not right."

Hubert gripped her shoulders and gave her a little shake. "Not right? Being apart isn't right." He cupped her chin. "Pearl, look at me. Look me in the eye and tell me you don't love me. Tell me, Pearl."

She tried to force her eyes to connect with Hubert's, but her heart couldn't comply with his demand. She turned away to stare into nothingness. "I can't marry you, Hubert."

Hubert's head dipped and angled to force her to look at him. "Pearl, my dear, being a Pinkerton detective for almost thirty years, I learned to read people's faces to see if they were telling the truth." He gently placed two fingers under her chin and tipped her head to face him. "Your eyes don't match your words."

Tightness in her throat prevented her from insisting he was wrong. Truth be told, he wasn't wrong, and she teetered on the brink of admitting as much. Just as her resolve began to topple, the kitchen door swung open and Silas Cain stood in the doorway.

"Say, what's going on in here?"

She never resented an intrusion more than she did at that very moment.

## twelve

"Nothing is going on, Silas." Pearl's eyes lingered on Hubert as she spoke. She'd never seen him with such an angry glare as the one he threw in her boarder's direction. The steely determination in his eyes made her catch her breath, and she forced herself to turn and look at the man standing in the kitchen doorway.

Silas took two steps forward. "Is this man bothering you?"

"Now, see here, Cain. . ." Icicles hung on Hubert's tone, and Pearl felt his hand tense on her arm. Surely they wouldn't come to blows!

"Gentlemen." Pearl stepped away from Hubert and held up both hands, a palm in each of their directions. "It's been a long day. I'm tired, and I must ask both of you to—" She glanced toward Hubert. The words *leave me alone* refused to cross her lips, so she turned back to her boarder. "Silas, please go back to the parlor. Everything here is fine."

Silas scowled at Hubert and grumbled under his breath but turned on his heel and strode out of the kitchen.

As soon as she looked fully at Hubert, she knew it was a mistake. His image so impacted her, she felt as though his arms encircled her, gently holding her close, even though he stood three paces away. "Good night, Hubert."

"Pearl, I'm not going to give up. I intend to keep coming back until you understand how much I love you, and nothing, I mean absolutely nothing, is going to change that."

She couldn't look at him any longer. Her heartbeat thrummed in her ears, and her chest ached to tell him she loved him. Instead, she fixed her gaze on the worn worktable and dropped her voice to a whisper. "Please, Hubert. Don't make this any harder."

"Good night, Pearl. I'll be back."

The soft click of the door closing behind him as he exited sent a pang of grief through Pearl's heart. If only Hubert would treat her with contempt or respond in anger to her repeated insistence that she would not marry him, forgetting about him might be easier. But every time she saw him she noticed he looked pale and drawn with dark circles under his eyes, and pain filled his expression. She wasn't sure how much longer her resolve would remain intact, especially if Hubert fulfilled his promise to return.

Fickle emotions warred within her as she poured out the lukewarm tea. Her fingers traced the blue flowers on the teapot Hubert had brought. How like him to do something like that. As adamant as she was about her decision, deep inside she wanted Hubert to come back, and she knew her heart wasn't ready to let go. A groan escaped.

"I can't keep doing this." She covered her face with her hands. "God, please help me put my feelings for Hubert aside and remember why I made this choice in the first place."

"What choice is that, Pearl?"

She startled and yanked her hands away from her face. Silas once again stood in the kitchen doorway. Ire bristled in her middle.

"Silas, must you sneak into my kitchen that way?"

A smooth, self-confident smile slid into place on his countenance. "I wasn't sneaking, Pearl. I was merely checking to make sure you were all right." He tossed a casual glance toward the back door. "Wasn't that the fellow who works in the mercantile?"

Pearl narrowed her eyes at her boarder. "Silas, is there something you need, or are you just trying to irritate me?"

He held one hand over his heart, and his disbelieving expression mocked her. "Why Pearl, I'm hurt. Here I come to check on your safety and well-being, and you accuse me of an ulterior motive."

If her emotions weren't already so ragged, she might have snorted at his ridiculous statement. The only part of her in danger in Hubert's presence was her heart, but she had no intention of discussing Hubert with Silas.

She pulled her shoulders back and picked up her dish towel. "As you can see, I'm just fine. Now please excuse me so I can finish up my chores. I'd like to turn in early."

"Pearl. . ." Silas closed the space between them and took the towel out of her hands. "May we talk?"

Was he *trying* to provoke her? "Can't it wait? I still have much to do to finish my work."

He laid the dish towel on the worktable. "I apologize, Pearl, but I truly cannot wait another minute. I must speak with you."

She tried unsuccessfully to stifle a sigh. "All right. What is so important that it can't wait until morning?"

Silas gestured toward one of the kitchen chairs. If weariness wasn't climbing her frame she might have chosen to stand just to be contrary. Immediately she chided herself. Whatever was on his mind was important to him, and God didn't want her behaving in such a petulant manner. Besides, the sooner he spoke his piece, the sooner he would leave her alone with her thoughts. She crossed to the chair and sat, clasping her hands in her lap. Raising a questioning look, she waited for him to speak.

He cleared his throat. "Pearl, as you know, I am a successful entrepreneur, working with an investment company out of St. Louis and Chicago."

He'd already told her as much the day he showed up on her doorstep. She supposed his point in repeating the declaration was to impress her. But she wasn't impressed. "I believe you've mentioned that."

Silas tugged at his brocade vest. "I am in the process of acquiring certain properties that, once in my hands, will become growing enterprises with the potential to. . .well, let's just say I will have the ability to live *very* comfortably."

She frankly didn't care a fig about Silas's investments and couldn't understand why he felt the need to share the information with her. If all he wanted was to brag to her about his soon-coming wealth, she wasn't waiting to hear any more. She started to rise.

"Silas, I—"

"Wait, Pearl, please." He took a long stride, his polished boots stopping inches from her own scuffed but sturdy button shoes. She plopped back onto the chair. Before she could draw another breath, he lowered himself to one knee and enfolded her hands between his.

"Pearl, it grieves me to see you work yourself into exhaustion day after day. I can see to it that you won't ever have to work another day in your life. Marry me, Pearl."

❧

Pearl picked up the silver music box and sat on the edge of her bed. As promised, Hubert had come by each evening, patiently but persistently trying to persuade her to tell him the reason she'd broken their engagement and assuring her of his love. With each visit, she felt her resolve weaken. She'd forced the words, telling him not to come back, but he'd just kept repeating that her eyes didn't agree with what she was saying. How could she continue to send him away when her heart throbbed in anticipation of seeing him?

She gently turned the key on the side of the music box two full revolutions, and she lifted the lid. The sweet, plaintive notes of Strauss's haunting melody engraved their print on her soul. Last night she thought if she returned the music box to Hubert he would accept that as her final word. But he refused to take it, and now relief pushed anxiety out of the way. Only God knew how much she treasured Hubert's engagement gift. She closed her eyes and invited the memory of Hubert's proposal—a foolish use of her time since it only intensified her anguish. But instead of Hubert's face, the unexpected recollection of Silas getting down on one knee imposed itself in her mind. She frowned and shook her head.

For the past three days, Silas had watched her expectantly. She could feel his eyes following her as she moved about the dining room serving meals or clearing the table. Every time he poked his head into the kitchen she'd made certain her hands were busy. Thankfully, he left the boardinghouse each morning after breakfast to conduct his business—whatever it was. She closed the lid on the music box and returned the treasure to her bedside table, unwilling to allow the memory of Silas's proposal to be accompanied by Hubert's music.

She'd tried to tell him her answer while he was still on his knee, but he'd laid his finger over her lips and told her to think about it. She could still picture the way his eyebrows dipped, as though he were admonishing a child, when he told her not to keep him waiting too long for her answer.

"Think about it! *Pfft*. There's nothing to think about. I tried to tell him, and he wouldn't let me."

She stood and straightened her shoulders, determination pressing her lips together. She had work to do. Gathering her mop and dust cloth, she headed upstairs to clean the boarders' rooms.

A prick on her conscious snagged her attention. After Everett had come to the boardinghouse to see her, she'd spent nearly the entire night in prayer. She'd begged God to direct her. But she had to admit, to herself and to God, that she'd not had peace about her decision to end her engagement to Hubert. She'd reached the conclusion on her own and did not wait for assurance from God. "What other choice did I have? How could I be content with Hubert knowing I'd contributed to his unhappiness, coming between him and his son?"

She reached the first bedroom at the top of the stairs and began running her dust cloth over the furniture. Her tasks were so routine she could perform them without thought. She pushed her mop back and forth across the floor, straightening items as she went. Moving to the next room— Silas's room—she blew out a stiff breath of annoyance and plunged into her chore.

A messy array of papers cluttered the top of the bureau. She picked them up to dust and one fell to the floor. She put the rest into a tidy stack and bent to retrieve the one that had fallen. As she laid it with the others, however, her eye caught her own name written toward the bottom. She hesitated a moment. Reading the paper would be an invasion of Silas's privacy, wouldn't it? But if her name was on this paper, didn't she have the right to know why?

Her gaze scanned the paper. It was a letter to a man named Wendall. Judging by the tone of the letter, Pearl assumed he was one of the business associates Silas was always talking about. As she read further, she gasped.

*As far as Pearl Dunnigan goes, I'm wearing her down.*
*She has been rather stubborn, but it shouldn't take too much*
*longer until her property is in my possession. I will employ*
*whatever means are necessary in order to. . .*

She heard the front door open and close.
"Pearl?"
*Silas.* What was he doing here in the middle of the day? She folded the paper and jammed it into her apron pocket, clenched her teeth, and exited the room. With each footfall

on the stairs her indignation grew, but she mustn't allow Silas to know she had read the letter. Not yet.

"Silas, I'm surprised to see you in the middle of the day. I thought your business kept you occupied."

A glib smile creased his face. "There you are." He met her at the bottom of the stairs with a bouquet of wildflowers in his hand, but she ignored him and the flowers and immediately turned toward the kitchen. As she assumed he would, Silas followed her. She took a wooden bowl from the shelf, then walked purposefully to the pantry to fetch a crock of lard and an assortment of spices. "What are you doing here, Silas?" She set the items on the worktable and returned to the pantry for a basket of apples.

"Well Pearl, that's rather insensitive. . ." He stepped out of her way as she pushed the basket onto the table. "Seeing as how I've given you three whole days. . ."

She reached in a drawer and drew out a large knife. Silas backed up and moved to the other side of the table.

"Pearl, I simply cannot wait any longer. You've kept me in suspense long enough. I must know your answer."

Pearl picked up an apple, quartered it, and began peeling the sections without looking at him. The oversized blade made the chore a bit awkward, but she didn't bother trading the knife for a smaller, less intimidating one. "Silas, if you recall, I tried to give you my answer the other night, but you wouldn't let me."

"W–well, I know that. . .ladies. . .need time to think things over."

She selected another apple from the basket and paused, her knife poised. "I didn't need time to think it over at all." She pushed the blade through the fruit and split it into halves and then into quarters. "But now I am actually glad I had time to consider the whole matter, because a new issue has come to light." Slivers of red peelings dropped into the wooden bowl. "My answer to your proposal shouldn't surprise you. It was *no* seven years ago, it was *no* three nights ago, and it's still *no*." She sliced the apple into thin pieces.

"But Pearl, how can you cast aside such an opportunity? Think of what it would mean for us, for you. This house—"

Pearl jerked her head up and shot a pointed look at him. "You were saying something about *my* house?"

He blinked and hesitated, as though rearranging his words. "Well yes, of course it's your house. That's beside the point." He came around the side of the table, eyeing her knife as he did so. "You can't continue to operate this house, this business, alone. Just think of how hard you work every day, the arduous duties, the drudgery. You shouldn't have to do this. Marry me, Pearl."

She sucked in a deep breath. "Silas, I've already given you my answer, and I don't plan to change it. But there is still one other matter to address." Before he could argue further, she pulled the letter from her apron pocket.

Silas's face turned purple and the veins popped out on his neck. He reached for the paper, but Pearl yanked it back out of his reach.

"That's my personal business. You have no right to—"

"I was cleaning your room and this fell on the floor. You should really be more careful what you leave lying around, Silas."

His icy glare and twitching jaw defined his anger, but Pearl refused to be intimidated.

"It appears the only reason you wanted me to marry you was so you could"—she unfolded the letter and glanced at it—"take possession of my property."

A sound akin to a growl emanated from Silas's throat. "It's against the law to read other people's mail."

"It's also against the law to defraud someone of their property." She tucked the letter back into her pocket. "And this wasn't in the mail yet. It was a paper in a room in *my house* that I was cleaning."

She picked up another apple and sliced it in half. "You have five minutes to pack your things and leave this house. Otherwise, I'm going to the sheriff."

It felt good to state emphatically what she felt, but judging by the thunderclouds forming in his eyes and the sneer on his lips, Silas wasn't finished. "You'll be sorry you did this, Pearl. I'm used to getting what I want."

# thirteen

Streaks of pink and gold painted the eastern sky, but Hubert had been up for hours. Sipping his third cup of coffee, he stood at his front window and watched the morning yawn and stretch its arms over the treetops that hugged the outline of the boardinghouse. He'd not told Pearl about Everett's decision to go back East. If their relationship was to be renewed, it had to be because Pearl loved him, not because Everett was leaving, if that was the reason she'd broken the engagement in the first place. He shrugged. She'd learn about Everett's departure eventually. Besides, if the news Silas Cain had told him yesterday in the store was true, she might not care anyway.

"Lord, I've made so many wrong decisions over the years, but I still feel Pearl is the woman You have chosen for me. If that's true, won't You please change her mind?"

He heard Everett stirring in his room. Probably packing his bag before coming out for breakfast. How Hubert wished he could convince his son to stay in Willow Creek. Having spent the predawn hours in prayer, Hubert rested in the assurance that God would work out every detail according to His pleasure. A smile lifted one corner of his lips. There was comfort in knowing the outcome wasn't up to him.

"Lord, You are worthy of my trust. You've proven Yourself faithful so many times, even when I didn't deserve Your mercy. Instead of telling You what I want, I'd rather just remain close to You and see what Your will has in store for me and Pearl. . .and Everett."

The door to Everett's room opened. Hubert turned with

his coffee mug in hand. Everett was dressed in his traveling clothes, and a valise of fine, tooled leather dangled from his hand. Disappointment pierced Hubert's heart once more, and he sent a quick prayer heavenward, asking for the fortitude to bid his son good-bye.

"Good morning, son. Would you like eggs for breakfast?"

Everett set the bag down and crossed to the kitchen. "No thank you. Just coffee."

"Let me make a fresh pot." Hubert wrapped a kitchen towel around the handle of the coffeepot and dumped the grounds into the bucket by the dry sink.

"I don't want you to go to any trouble." Resignation replaced the haughtiness that had laced Everett's voice a few weeks ago.

How could he make Everett understand that doing little things for him was a pleasure, not an imposition? "It's no trouble, son." Hubert rinsed out the pot and then pumped fresh water into it, adding the freshly ground coffee. There was plenty of time. The stage wasn't due for another three hours.

While the coffee's aroma wafted through the room, Everett withdrew his watch and checked it, then tucked it back into his vest pocket.

Hubert studied his son "You know it's not too late to change your mind."

Everett pulled out a chair and sat at the table. "I spent the night listening to you pace out here." He shifted in his chair. "I couldn't sleep either."

"I'm sorry if I kept you awake."

Everett shook his head. "You didn't. I had so many things on my mind, it was hard to close my eyes." He looked at Hubert. "It doesn't seem that we've been able to resolve our differences, but perhaps it's not as much your fault as I once thought."

If Everett was willing to initiate further discussion on the matter, Hubert was ready to listen. "Did you come to any conclusions?"

His son rose and walked to the front window where Hubert had stood watching the sunrise a few minutes earlier. "I'm not sure." Hubert heard him sigh. "But I wasn't sure when I came to Willow Creek either. I thought I knew what my purpose in coming was, but now. . ."

Hubert checked the coffeepot and returned to sit at the table. "You know I want you to stay, but it's your choice. Do you have plans?"

Everett blew out a breath and turned away from the window. He extracted an envelope from his inside coat pocket. "I received this letter from Grandfather's attorney last week." He stared at the envelope, a scowl marring his features. "I was unaware of the unpaid debts and liens against Grandfather's business."

Surprise at Everett's statement raised Hubert's eyebrows. Everett had told him he stood to inherit a great deal of money and planned to take over his grandfather's business, but it sounded as though bad news from the attorney might change his son's future.

Everett unfolded the missive and studied it silently. Judging from his son's slumped shoulders, Hubert suspected he'd already read it several times.

Everett held the letter up, waving it slightly. "At first I didn't plan to share this information with you. I didn't want you to know."

Hubert frowned, not in anger but in puzzlement.

Everett shuffled over and sat at the table again, laying the letter in front of him. "But there is something here you *should* know."

Hubert cut his gaze to the letter. Several pages lay on the table, so whatever explanation it contained was lengthy.

"This lawyer, Mr. Goss, was originally my grandmother's attorney. She hired him to handle some legal affairs involving my mother. After Grandmother died, Mr. Goss contacted my grandfather, who retained him at that point. He says that he was under obligation to my grandfather to keep this information confidential until now." Everett stared at the letter with doleful eyes. "It seems we were wrong about not knowing where my mother went."

Hubert blinked and raised his eyebrows. "But we *didn't* know."

"Grandmother did." He looked across the table at his father. "And on more than one occasion, she wired money to my mother—large amounts of money." He turned the pages over. "By the time we got word of Mother's death, Grandmother had sent almost a hundred thousand dollars to her. Mr. Goss says the bank drafts were sent to various places and cashed at different banks, and he suspects the man with whom Mother ran away may have been blackmailing her." His fingers curled up the corners of the pages and his eyes remained riveted to the paper.

Hubert tried to digest the staggering information. "You mean. . ."

"Mother's leaving wasn't entirely your fault." Everett leaned his head back and blew out his breath through pursed lips. "I wanted to keep on blaming you. Grandmother always told me you weren't a good man; you weren't good enough for my mother." He thumped his open palm down onto the letter. "But I blamed you based on her word, without knowing the facts."

Hubert shook his head. "It sounds like none of us knew the facts."

A grim line defined Everett's lips. "Except Grandmother. After she died, Mr. Goss had to tell Grandfather about the missing money as well as several large bills my grandmother ran up without his knowledge. At some point, and the letter isn't completely clear on this, Grandfather signed over 51 percent ownership of the business to Grandmother. She apparently used Grandfather's business as collateral for loans, sending the money to my mother. Mr. Goss is in the process of sorting out the details of settling the estate, but the house and furnishings may have to be sold to pay off the creditors. Grandfather's business is in receivership."

Hubert stood to retrieve the coffeepot that had begun to boil. "Since you may not have a house to go back to, why don't you stay here?"

Another sigh hung on the air as Everett refolded the letter and tucked it back into his coat pocket. "You've made a life for yourself in this place, but Iowa isn't where I belong."

"It could be." Hubert poured two cups of coffee and set one before Everett. "I have a comfortable home and the mercantile. I know it's not the life to which you are accustomed, but—"

Everett waved his hand and took a sip of coffee. "Mr. Goss indicates he will have some papers for me to sign and there should be a small inheritance after all the creditors are paid. I'm afraid it will be a fraction of what I was expecting, but at least it's something. Once I return to Baltimore, I'll weigh my options."

"Couldn't Willow Creek be one of your options?"

Everett hesitated before answering. "No, Father. I have no future here. I hope you can find happiness in Willow Creek, but I think it's best if I leave."

≈

Since Everett needed the wagon to carry his trunk and his valise, Hubert had taken his time walking to the mercantile. The normal sounds of Willow Creek's commerce that usually brought a smile to his lips failed to cheer him this morning. The sun hid behind gloomy gray clouds that matched Hubert's melancholy mood. He puttered around the store, waited on a half dozen customers, and opened a crate of merchandise. When the clock on the shelf behind the counter chimed, Hubert pulled out his watch, thinking the clock must surely be running fast. But the hands of his watch confirmed it was nearly time to bid Everett good-bye.

He hung the CLOSED sign on the mercantile door and walked down the street to meet Everett at the depot before the stage arrived. As painful as it was, he'd not let his son leave without telling him one more time that he loved him and wanted him to stay.

Everett stood beside his valise and trunk on the boardwalk in front of the depot. There wasn't much left to say, other than repeating what had already been spoken. Hubert opened his mouth to entreat his son one last time to stay in Willow Creek when he heard a shout from down the street. He'd hoped on this day the stage might arrive late, thus giving him extra time with Everett. But instead, the conveyance must be pulling into town early. They both looked in the direction of the noise.

Within moments, more people added their voices to the shouting, and Hubert realized it wasn't the stage's arrival. Some kind of commotion drew the attention of nearly everyone on the street. Several folks ran toward the clamor. Just as he turned to see what was happening, he saw billows of smoke rising above the trees, and one of the men yelled over his shoulder as he ran.

"The boardinghouse is on fire!"

Horror gripped Hubert by the throat. He forced his brain to function and his feet to move. Down the alley was a shorter route. With his heart pounding in his ears and his chest constricting, he ran toward Pearl's place.

"God, let her get out of there. Please let her be safe."

He was vaguely aware of footsteps hammering out a rhythm behind him in step with his own.

"Father!"

When he reached the yard of the boardinghouse, men were already manning the pump, working the handle up and down with ferocity. Others carried buckets and burlap sacks.

But where was Pearl? His eyes darted from one side of the yard to the other. "Pearl!"

He raced to the front of the house. No Pearl, but the curtains at the parlor window were already in flames. Yelling Pearl's name at the top of his lungs, he elbowed past the lilac bushes. There was no answer. His frantic search brought him back where he'd started. Pearl was nowhere outside.

As he pushed past the men who had formed a line, slinging water buckets, the crackle of the fire reached his ears. Dense smoke nearly blotted out the location of the back door.

"Pearl!"

Without hesitation, Hubert lunged toward the door. Several hands grabbed at him, and a conglomeration of voices accosted his senses—urgent entreaties for him to not enter the burning house.

"Stay back! Don't go in there!"

"Are you crazy, man? You won't come out of there alive."

He yanked his arms free of the restraining grips and pushed forward. Another voice pierced through the commotion.

"No, Father! Stop!"

But he couldn't stop. His feet, propelled by a force he didn't see, carried him past the porch steps. A degree of strength he'd never known before sent jolts of energy through him.

"Pearl!"

A roiling wall of black smoke met him when he flung the door open. He raised his arm, waving the deadly veil away, and covered his face in the crook of his elbow. "Pearl!. . . Pearl!"

He plunged into the kitchen. The smoke drove him to

his knees. It unfurled against him from every side, and he couldn't determine the direction from which the fire came. The thick vapor was denser near the ceiling, but lower down he could make out the forms of the kitchen table and chairs, the legs of the cast-iron stove, the bottom edge of the pantry door. He tried to scream out Pearl's name again, but black fog that tasted like tar burned his throat. If he'd taken a moment to wet a cloth and tie it over the lower half of his face, he might be able to breathe easier, but the action would have taken several precious seconds, and he didn't know how many seconds he had to find Pearl. He pulled his shirt up to cover his nose and mouth, and continued crawling through the kitchen, but Pearl wasn't there.

"P–p. . .earl." Spasms of coughing choked him. The sound of the crackling grew louder and something crashed behind him. "P–p—" Impenetrable smoke wrapped virulent fingers around his throat. He could no longer push Pearl's name past his lips, but his heart continued to scream. Only God could hear him. Heat intensified moment by moment, but awareness of time began to slip away. Coughs tore at his windpipe and wracked his chest.

*Pearl, my love, where are you? God, please show me where she is. Lead me to her.*

His shoulder came in contact with something solid, and it fell over with a thud that joined with the growing cacophony of the fire. He crawled blindly, unable to open his eyes to the searing heat and smoke. Something scraped and toppled behind him. From the same direction he'd come? He couldn't tell. Another thump and a knocking sound reached him. Somewhere a window shattered and an ominous cracking and splintering of wood meant the beams would soon collapse.

*Please Father, lead me to Pearl.*

With his hand he groped to the right of him and

encountered a wall, then an opening. A doorway. He stretched his arm and probed farther through the recess. His fingers floundered in the space and collided with warm softness lying on the floor just inside the door.

His lips formed the word *Pearl*, even though he couldn't force out any sound. He'd found her, but darkness entombed him and his sense of where he was in the house began to slip away. Locking his hand around her limp arm, he tried to drag her. A sensation of lightness overpowered him and took possession of his ability to think. The urgency that drove him into the house faded as oppressive heat enveloped him. His last shred of strength withered and died. The demon smoke was swallowing them, and they were falling. . .falling. . .

# fourteen

Hubert fought to breathe through a snarled labyrinth of cobwebs, seeking an escape from the burning in his throat. Muffled voices called his name and encouraged him to open his eyes. Part of him desired to push his way through the fog and another part simply wanted to sleep. Could he find the strength to open his mouth and tell whoever was repeating his name to go away? A searing pain knifed his throat when he swallowed. He turned his head to one side and met gentle fingers touching his cheek and blotting his face with something blessedly cool.

"Mr. Behr, can you hear me?"

The voice sounded familiar, but he couldn't connect a name or face to it. If responding to the entreaty intensified the pounding in his head, perhaps lying perfectly still was his best option. His lips refused to cooperate when he tried to form the question *Where am I?*

"Don't try to talk. Just open your mouth and take a sip of water."

*Water.* The very word sounded heavenly. He parted his lips, and his bottom lip cracked painfully. He pulled his eyebrows in as a wince filled his whole being. But an instant later, cool water dripped into his mouth and quenched some of the pain. His tongue, thick and swollen, detached itself from the roof of his mouth and relished the wetness. Gradual awareness seeped into his brain. Whoever held the cup to his lips poured a tiny bit more water into his mouth, and Hubert let the precious moisture roll over his tongue. Since his first attempt to swallow was so painful, he wasn't anxious to repeat the experience. He mentally braced himself and allowed his swallow reflex to work. As expected, it felt like pouring kerosene on an open wound.

"I know your throat hurts, but the doctor said you must try to take some water."

Understanding finally broke through. The voice belonged to Hannah Vogel, the doctor's wife. Most people just called her Mrs. Doc. Along with the realization of who ministered to him came the horrific memory of crawling through the burning boardinghouse. Shred by shred, the picture came together.

Footsteps scurried away from where he lay, and he heard Mrs. Doc's voice again. "Mr. Behr is awake." Heavier footsteps accompanied those of the town doctor's diminutive wife.

"Hubert? It's Doc Vogel. Can you hear me?"

Hubert fought past the pain and tried to force his lips to work. Was there enough air in his lungs to push a single word out? "P. . .P. . ." He reached deep within himself for the determination to speak. The word came out as a hoarse whisper. "Pearl."

The doctor's fingers forced one of Hubert's eyes open, then the other. The air stung his eyes and they watered, blurring the image of the doctor. "Let's take a listen." Doc laid an instrument on Hubert's chest and moved it around several times before he seemed satisfied.

"Mm-hm. Mm-hm." Doc thumped his fingertips on Hubert's chest. "Has he coughed yet?"

Mrs. Doc answered in the negative. "But he has swallowed a few sips of water."

"Good. Let's sit him up." The two pairs of hands grasped his arms and shoulders and pulled him forward. His head swam, and the cot on which he lay floated like a leaf on an air current. Hubert opened his eyes again, tiny slits, enough to see Doc and Mrs. Doc standing on either side of him. Mrs. Doc moved to stuff pillows behind him. Then they leaned him back on the pillows and after several moments, the room stopped swaying like a runaway stagecoach.

"Pearl." It hurt to even whisper, but his concern for Pearl outdistanced his own discomfort.

"Hubert, I want you to try and cough. It's going to hurt, but you need to expel that bad air in your lungs. We don't want you developing pneumonia."

Why wouldn't Doc tell him about Pearl?

Hubert commanded his eyes to open as wide as he could make them. He wrapped his fingers around Doc's wrist. "Pearl."

Doc's grave expression sent shards of fear through him. "She's in the next room. She hasn't awakened yet. I'm afraid she took in quite a bit of smoke, and she has a few burns on her arm and hand."

Hubert tightened his grip involuntarily, and the doctor's expression softened. "If she wakes up in the next few hours, and if we can get her to sit up and cough like we are trying to do with you, I'll have a better idea of her prognosis. But right now, the best one I can give you is *guarded*."

Hubert gave the doctor a nod. Even the muscles in his neck and shoulders ached. A cough climbed up his tortured windpipe. He tried to hold it back, but it burst forth with lancing pain. Once he started coughing, he couldn't stop and the spasms wracked his chest. Perspiration collected on his face. Mrs. Doc continued to blot the damp cloth over his brow until the throes of coughing subsided. Exhausted, he leaned back against the pillows.

Doc Vogel listened to Hubert's chest again. "I know it hurts, but you need to cough." He pulled up a chair and sat next to Hubert's cot. "You probably have some questions, and since speaking is difficult, I'm going to guess what those questions are and answer them the best I can."

Hubert locked eyes with the doctor, hoping to communicate his concern over Pearl. He remembered finding her but not pulling her out of the house. How had they gotten out? "Nobody knows yet how the fire started, but the sheriff is still poking around over there. You and Mrs. Dunnigan were both unconscious when you were pulled out. The flames broke through the wall, and the place was starting to collapse." Doc leaned forward and put his hand on Hubert's shoulder. "If it wasn't for your son pulling both of you out of there when he did, we'd be burying you today. He pulled you out first, then went back in for Miss Pearl. He even had the presence of mind to roll her in a rug. Otherwise, her burns would have been much worse."

*Everett pulled Pearl and me out? I didn't even realize he'd followed me into the house.* With the memory of the harrowing trek through the smoke-filled boardinghouse, more pieces fell into place. He recalled hearing something thump behind him. Was that Everett?

The idea of Everett saving not only his life but Pearl's as well sank in. With the realization came fear for his son's condition. "Ever–ett." He pushed out the hoarse croak.

Doc Vogel's brow knitted into furrows. "He has some pretty nasty burns. Before the laudanum took effect, he kept asking if he had gotten to you and Mrs. Dunnigan in time."

More coughing seized Hubert, and he fought his way through the spasm. "How bad. . .Everett?"

Doc shook his head. "Well, he didn't swallow too much smoke because he'd tied a wet rag over his mouth and nose. Unfortunately, parts of his clothing caught fire when the ceiling caved in. I'm not going to lie to you, some of his burns are serious. But if we can keep infection from setting in, he has a good chance."

Hubert slumped back onto the pillows. Everett saved his

and Pearl's lives at the risk of his own. It was a staggering revelation. But Doc continued to fill in the blanks.

"One of the men who helped fight the fire said Mrs. Dunnigan had come out, but then she ran back in before anyone could stop her. When your son pulled her out of the house, she had a silver music box in her hands. I had to pry her fingers away from it."

❧

Her head throbbed and wracking pain filled her chest and throat, but Pearl opened her eyes to find a small mountain of pillows behind her back and shoulders, and Hannah Vogel bathing her face. As soon as the doctor's wife realized Pearl was awake, a huge smile split her face. "Oh, thank the good Lord. We've been praying for you for two days." The woman hurried to the doorway and called her husband, then returned to Pearl's bedside.

Doc Vogel's smile matched his wife's when he saw Pearl. "You certainly gave us a scare, young lady." He immediately poked the ends of his stethoscope into his ears and listened to her chest.

Young lady? Mercy sakes, who did he think he was talking to? She started to open her mouth, but the doctor stopped her.

"No, no. Don't try to speak." He flipped the stethoscope around his neck. "You suffered some burns in your throat from breathing in the hot air. The smoke caused some damage, too. You've already coughed up some blood. That's why we have you propped up like this."

He motioned for his wife to bring a lamp closer, and he stuck a piece of flat wood in her mouth. The doctor frowned and made some grunting sounds as he peered inside. "Well, your throat is still swollen, but it's showing signs of healing. Until it heals completely, I don't want you to talk at all. Drink sips of water, as much as you can, and Hannah will help you gargle with some salt water later." He patted her shoulder.

When she tried to raise her arm, a sharp pain jolted her, and she noticed the bandages on her left hand and arm. Doc Vogel partially unwrapped one of the bandages and peered beneath it. "The burns aren't too serious. In a few days you won't need the bandages any longer. I'm more concerned with the burns in your throat." He gently replaced the swathing around her hand.

Pearl tried to mouth words, but the doctor kept admonishing her to keep silent. She held up her hands, palms facing each other, a few inches apart, and Hannah brightened.

"I think I know what she wants." The woman went to a small bureau and opened the top drawer. When she turned, she had Pearl's music box in her hands. "Is this it?"

Relief filled her. The box looked a bit tarnished but otherwise unscathed. She reached out for the cherished treasure.

"You have a couple of visitors. Mr. Behr has been in the next room asking about you ever since he regained consciousness yesterday."

The peculiar statement took Pearl aback. Hubert regained consciousness? Puzzlement must have shown on her face because Mrs. Doc hurriedly explained that Hubert was pulled out of the burning boardinghouse along with her. It still didn't make sense.

Doc Vogel instructed his wife to give Pearl sips of water, as much as she would take. Then he turned back to Pearl. "The sheriff has been waiting to talk to you. He can tell you everything that happened, at least what he knows so far. Do you feel up to a visit with him?"

Confusion boggled her mind. She vaguely remembered the fire but didn't recall Hubert being there. Why were they telling her Hubert had been pulled from the burning house? Was he all right? And why did the sheriff want to speak with her?

Doc Vogel went to the door and motioned with his hand. Sheriff Webster stepped into the room and removed his hat. He was a pleasant sort, and although he'd only been in Willow Creek for a little over a year, she knew Hubert liked him.

"Ma'am. I'm sure pleased to see you doin' better, and I apologize for intrudin' like this while you're recoverin'."

The doctor brought a chair for the sheriff to sit next to Pearl's cot and waggled a warning finger at the lawman. "I don't want you upsetting her or tiring her out. She is not allowed to speak. If you have a question that she can't answer by nodding or shaking her head, it'll have to wait."

"Is she allowed to write?"

Doc scowled. "If it's absolutely necessary." He told his wife to find a tablet and pencil, then turned back to the sheriff. "My wife is going to stay in here, and if she thinks Miss Pearl needs to rest, your visit is over."

Sheriff Webster agreed. "This shouldn't take too long. Mrs. Dunnigan, I do have a few questions."

Frustration seethed inside her. She had some questions, too, and as soon as Hannah Vogel put paper and pencil in her hands, she intended to ask them.

"First of all, do you have any idea how the fire started?" Pearl shook her head.

"Were you inside the house when you realized it was on fire?"

She nodded. Hannah finally reentered the room with paper and pencil, and handed them to Pearl.

"Did you notice anyone hangin' around the boardinghouse?"

Pearl started writing, but her pencil scrawls had nothing to do with the sheriff's question. *Why was Hubert unconscious? What was he doing there?* She handed the tablet to the sheriff.

"Well, he went into the house after you. He was hollerin' your name." The sheriff gave her a tiny half smile. "Only a crazy man would run into a burnin' house, unless he's lookin' for someone. In that case, I reckon he's in love."

She reached for the tablet and scribbled another question. *Is he all right?* When she shoved the paper back at the sheriff, he nodded and widened his smile.

"I reckon so. I was just talkin' to him a little bit ago. Funny, he keeps askin' the same question about you."

Relief washed over her. Her Hubert had risked his life trying to save her. Thank God he was all right.

"Ma'am? Do you mind if I ask some of my questions now, 'fore Doc comes back in here and throws me out?"

Hannah snickered over in the corner as she poured fresh water into a cup. Pearl nodded at the sheriff, blinking back grateful tears.

"Ma'am, did you happen to notice Everett Behr anywhere around the boardinghouse that morning?"

She nodded.

The lawman frowned. "You did. Do you know what he was doin'?"

She nodded again and picked up the pencil. *Came to see me.*

A peculiar expression fell across Sheriff Webster's face. "Did he threaten you in any way?"

Pearl shook her head. What was this about? Everett might not like her, but she was fairly certain he'd never physically harm her.

"When he came to see you, what did he want?"

She set the pencil in motion again. *Apologized and said good-bye.*

The sheriff rubbed his bristly chin and chewed on his lip for a moment. Before he could ask Pearl to expound on her statement, she scratched out another note. *Find Silas Cain.* She nudged the note toward the sheriff and Hannah gently suggested that Pearl needed to rest and he could come back tomorrow. She shooed him out the door. After the woman gave Pearl a few sips of water, she told her to rest and slipped out, leaving the door ajar. The voices of Sheriff Webster and Doc Vogel drifted into the room from the hallway.

"How much do you know about Everett Behr?"

Doc harrumphed. "He's Hubert's son. Lived back East, Baltimore, I think. He's been in town for about a month or so. Why?"

"What else do you know about him? Did he have any disagreements with anyone?"

Pearl heard Doc snort. "Only if you count Hubert and Pearl. I don't think he knew any other folks hereabouts. But some say he came to Willow Creek to stop the wedding between his father and Miss Pearl."

"That a fact?"

"Fact? I can't attest to any gossip I hear being fact. But there is one thing I know for sure: shortly after Everett Behr arrived in town, Pearl and Hubert stopped seeing each other."

Pearl wished she could see the men's faces. What was the sheriff getting at? As if he could read her thoughts through the wall that separated them, Sheriff Webster spoke again.

"There's rumors afoot that maybe Everett Behr set the fire. I talked with a few folks who gave me statements that the young fella didn't especially like Mrs. Dunnigan. Some say he was the reason she and Hubert Behr cancelled their weddin'. What I can't figure out is why."

"Why indeed? Pearl Dunnigan is a fine lady. Just about everyone in town loves her."

A few moments of silence were followed by the sheriff's voice. "You know anything about Silas Cain?"

"Not much, other than the fact that he lived here several years ago. As I recall, he wanted to court Miss Pearl back then, but I don't think she wanted any part of that."

Pearl squirmed against her pillows, listening to the exchange.

Doc Vogel continued. "I remember Cain up and left town real sudden. Most folks thought it was kind of strange, seeing as how Cain had asked Miss Pearl to marry him, but one day he was here and the next day he was gone."

# fifteen

"When can I see my son?"

Though still raspy, Hubert's throat was better. Doc Vogel attributed the improvement to the fact that Hubert had pulled his shirt up over his face to block some of the smoke as he crawled through the burning house.

The doctor's thick brows bunched together into a shaggy caterpillar hovering over his eyes. "Hubert, I'm glad you're feeling better, but I let you go home yesterday thinking you could rest better in your own bed. Why aren't you home in bed?" He held up his hand. "Never mind. I already know the answer. My wife told me she had to shoo you away from Miss Pearl's door earlier." He beckoned Hubert toward his office. "Come and let me explain some things."

Grumbling to himself about simply wanting some answers, Hubert followed Doc to the cramped nook in the corner of what should have been the front parlor in the doctor's house. Medical books lined the shelf above the desk and neat stacks of papers sat ready for the doctor's attention. Doc pointed to the chair beside the desk, and Hubert took the cue and sat.

"Doc, all I want is to know how Pearl is doing. When will she wake up? How is Everett? Is there any infection? Is he still—"

"All right, I get the idea." Doc leaned back in his chair and crossed one leg over the other. He pulled off his spectacles and pinched the area between his eyes. "First of all, Miss Pearl is doing as well as can be expected. She has already awakened a few times since yesterday, but she is under strict orders not to speak. Her throat and lungs sustained more damage than yours because she was exposed to the smoke and heat longer, but her breathing is somewhat better today. And like I told you yesterday, she has a few minor burns."

Relief washed over Hubert at the doctor's assessment of Pearl's recovery. He closed his eyes and whispered a prayer of gratitude.

Doc added his "amen" to Hubert's. "We've been keeping your son as comfortable as possible with laudanum, which not only takes the edge off his pain but also lets him sleep." He rubbed a hand across his gray whiskers. "Burns can be pretty difficult to treat. The burned skin must be cleaned off, which is a very painful process."

Hubert winced involuntarily, empathy cramping his gut at the thought of what his son was enduring. Guilt gnawed at him as he pictured Everett following him into the burning house.

The doctor continued. "There are some who advocate treating burns by holding the burned area as close as possible to the fire until it blisters, then draining the fluid from the blisters to promote healing." He harrumphed. "I've always disagreed with that approach. Besides, most of Everett's burns were beyond the blister stage anyway."

Tears stung Hubert's eyes and his irritated throat constricted. "How long until you know when he will recover?"

Doc Vogel turned compassionate eyes on Hubert, his tone as gentle as a doctor's could be when delivering words a loved one didn't want to hear. "*If* he will recover, Hubert. He still must fight off infection. Without skin covering these large wounds, infection can set in very easily. Daily cleaning and removal of burned flesh, along with applying a carbolic acid salve, will give him the best chance. But it's going to take a miracle for him to pull through this without infection."

The weight of Doc's words slammed into Hubert, stealing his breath. *Father in heaven, please don't ask me to say good-bye to my son this way.*

"Can I see him? Sit with him?"

The doctor shook his head. "I'm sorry, Hubert. Since we're trying to prevent infection, it would be best if as few people as possible go near him just now."

A tap on the door drew their attention, and Mrs. Doc poked her head in. "Sorry to interrupt, but the sheriff is here looking for Mr. Behr."

Hubert nodded and as he rose, Doc stopped him. "Hubert, in another day or two, I'll let you go in and see your son—when he's a little more stable."

Hubert clasped Doc's hand. "You said we need a miracle. That's just what we'll pray for." He followed Hannah Vogel out to the front porch where he found Sheriff Webster leaning against the porch railing. The two men greeted each other.

The lawman took his hat off and ran a hand through his hair. "Mrs. Doc tells me that Miss Pearl is doin' some better today."

Hubert nodded. "I've only gotten to see her once for a few minutes, but she was asleep." The sooner he found out what the sheriff wanted, the sooner he could go sit with Pearl again. "What can I do for you, Sheriff?"

Webster hooked his thumbs in his belt and studied Hubert. "I need to know if you can vouch for your son's whereabouts before the fire broke out."

Hubert raised his eyebrows. "We had breakfast together, then I left the house to go open the mercantile. He still had to pack a few more things. I told him to use the wagon to take his trunk and bag to the depot. The stage wasn't due in until ten o'clock."

The sheriff's poker face revealed nothing, but past experience being on the other side of the investigation process told Hubert there was more to the man's question.

He coughed and cleared his throat. "What's this about, Sheriff?"

The man pulled a bandana from his back pocket and wiped the inside band of his hat. "Well, Hubert, it's no secret that your son doesn't like Miss Pearl. I'm tryin' to determine just how much he doesn't like her. There's been some talk. . . purely speculation, mind you, but I'm obliged to follow up on it."

Hubert pulled on his most professional investigator air. "Gossip is never a reliable source, as you well know. Investigations are based on facts. So let me remind you of a few facts." He raised his pointer finger. "Fact number one: Everett was at the depot when the fire started."

"Nope." Webster shook his head. "He was at the depot when the fire was *discovered*. We don't know how long it had been burning."

Hubert nodded. "All right, but let me remind you of fact number two: He was just as shocked as I was when people started yelling that the boardinghouse was on fire. Thirdly, he ran into that burning house, and finally, he not only pulled me out, he pulled Pearl out as well. Doc Vogel said he rolled her in a rug. Otherwise she would have been burned much worse. Does that sound like the actions of an arsonist?"

Webster nodded. "Yep, I'm takin' all that into consideration. But it's also a fact that shortly after Everett came to town, you and Miss Pearl broke off your engagement."

Nobody needed to remind Hubert of the painful truth, but he kept his stone face intact. "If you're insinuating that Everett caused the cancellation of the wedding, why would that make him a suspect in the fire?" The exchange was edging too close for Hubert to maintain his cool poise, and the tension made him cough. "What you're suggesting is preposterous. He saved Pearl's life, and mine, and was burned in the process." He gritted his teeth and fought to control the anger and anxiety colliding in his chest.

Webster scratched his head and slapped his hat in place.

"For what it's worth, I tend to agree with you. Was Everett's purpose in comin' to Willow Creek to stop the weddin'? If so, then why would he try to hurt Miss Pearl if the engagement was off?" He stuffed the bandana back in his pocket. "Makes no sense, but I have to ask, especially since Pearl herself told me that Everett was at the boardinghouse about an hour before the fire."

"What?" Hubert struggled through another coughing spasm. "When did she tell you this?" He tossed his professional posture to the wind.

"Yesterday." The sheriff pulled a folded paper from his shirt pocket. "When I asked her why he was there, she wrote this." He held out the missive.

Hubert unfolded the paper and scanned it. "Came to see me. Apologized and said good-bye." As he stared at Pearl's handwriting, it blurred and he sucked in a breath. "He went to apologize to Pearl?" He allowed his gaze to wander toward the door that led to where Everett lay unconscious. "What was he apologizing for?"

"The lady didn't say." He tucked the folded paper back into his shirt pocket. "Just so you know, I wanted to question Silas Cain, too."

Hubert yanked his attention back to the lawman. "So did you?"

"Would have." Webster pushed away from the porch railing. "He left on the westbound stage the day of the fire."

"He left?" Hands on hips, Hubert weighed this bit of information against another piece of news, unsure of whether to share it with the sheriff. Discomfort made him shuffle his feet. "I don't know if you're aware, but Cain came into the mercantile a few days ago. He told me he'd asked Pearl to marry him."

Webster's eyebrows rose. "Is that so?"

"That's what he said. I had gone to see Pearl one evening

last week, and while she and I were talking in the kitchen, Cain came out and asked if I was bothering her." Hubert rolled the entire scenario over in his mind. "Then the day before the fire, Cain came in the store and told me he'd proposed to her. As I recall, he didn't come in to buy anything. It was as if his mission was to inform me that he had a claim on Pearl."

He and Webster stared at each other. "Doesn't it seem odd to you that Cain would leave town without coming to see Pearl or even attempting to find out how the woman he planned to marry is doing?"

⋙

A vague awareness of not being alone stirred Pearl's consciousness. Did she hear a voice?

"Pearl, my love, I'm here. I will always be here. Nothing can keep me away."

She tried to swallow, but the pain in her throat reminded her where she was, and why. Sunlight from the nearby window coaxed her eyes open. The first image that captured her vision was Hubert, sitting by her cot with his knees pressed as close as he could get to the side of the bed. A smile lifted the corners of his mustache, and she realized her hand was enfolded within his. Sweet warmth washed over her, and she had no desire to pull her hand away.

"Ah, my Pearl. You've been such a sleepyhead." His fingers squeezed hers.

Hannah Vogel stood behind Hubert's shoulder. "This man of yours simply will not take no for an answer. I got tired of chasing him out of here, so I brought him a chair. Would you like a few sips of water, dear?"

Hannah's description of Hubert danced in her mind. *This man of yours. . .* She wanted to hear it again. Instead, she nodded at Hannah's offer of water.

With an air of efficiency, Hannah moved to retrieve the

water pitcher and fill a cup.

"Can I do that for her?" Hubert held out his hand for the cup.

"Humph! As if a man can do such a thing without making a mess."

Pearl could hear a hint of humor in Hannah's voice. She wished she could laugh but held her amusement inside. To her delight, Hannah passed the cup to Hubert.

"I'll be right outside the door if you need anything." Hannah tugged Pearl's covers up to her chin, then cocked an eyebrow at Hubert. "Don't you upset her now." She exited, leaving the door standing open.

"I don't think Mrs. Doc approves of me acting as your nurse." Hubert slipped his hand behind her head and helped her lean forward. Pearl started to reach for the cup, but Hubert held it gently to her lips. When he tipped the vessel, the cool water sloshed over the rim, dribbling down one cheek to her neck and wetting the neckline of her gown as well as the edge of the sheet.

"Oops!" Hubert scowled. "Sorry, my dear. Clumsy of me."

"Told you so." Hannah's voice drifted in from the hallway.

He pulled his handkerchief from his pocket and blotted her face and neck, ignoring the teasing from the doctor's wife. "Let's try this again."

Endeared by Hubert's efforts, she didn't bother to show him she was perfectly able to give herself a drink. This time he held his handkerchief under the cup. His second attempt was more successful, and Pearl swallowed, albeit painfully, several sips of water.

"There now," he said, triumph defining the timbre of his voice. He set the cup down on the bedside table, returned to his chair, and reclaimed her hand. "Doc tells me you aren't allowed to talk for another day or two, so if you want more water, just point, all right?"

She nodded. How good his hand felt around hers. She never wanted him to let go.

"Has anyone told you anything about the fire?"

She shrugged one shoulder and held her thumb and forefinger close together.

"A little bit?" His gray eyes darkened, reflecting the distress he obviously felt over the incident. Small wonder since he was pulled from the house after having gone inside to find her. How could she express to him her gratitude for saving her life?

"Well, maybe I can fill in some of the blanks." He coughed a bit, then began telling her of the progression of events.

She made a motion with her hand, indicating she wanted to write. Hubert picked up the pad and pencil from the bedside table and handed it to her. Her position propped up in the bed made it awkward, but she scrawled on the paper, *You saved my life,* and handed it to him.

"No, love. It wasn't me, though I tried. I searched all around the outside of the house, but I couldn't find you. I went in through the back door thinking you might be in the kitchen. The smoke was so thick I couldn't see a thing, so I crawled through the kitchen and into the hallway. I'm afraid I did a mighty poor job of rescuing you. Sheriff Webster tells me you had escaped from the house, but you ran back inside." He squeezed her hand. "That was foolish, my dear."

She shook her head and touched the music box that lay beside her on the blanket.

"We could get you another music box." The tenderness in his expression and tone communicated to her he wasn't really scolding. "I'm just grateful to God, and to Everett, that you're going to be all right."

Everett? What was he talking about? If she'd been surprised to learn of Hubert's presence in the burning house, his last statement completely took her aback. She sent him a quizzical look.

Tears formed in Hubert's eyes. "It was Everett. He followed me into the house and pulled both of us out."

She stared at him, wide-eyed, too stunned to respond.

"Sheriff told me Everett came by to see you that morning. I'm glad he came to apologize for his attitude."

She started to form words but stopped when her raw throat constricted painfully. A coughing spasm gripped her, but she shook her head and picked up the pencil again. *Apologized for insisting I break the engagement. Said he knew he was wrong.*

Pearl's coughing brought Hannah back into the room. The woman shook her finger at Hubert. "What did I tell you about upsetting her?" Hannah scurried to the bed and fussed over Pearl, giving her a sip of water.

When the spasm eased, Pearl watched as Hubert read the note she'd scrawled. A look of astonishment filled his face.

"He insisted. . . When was this?"

But Hannah pointed at Hubert like a strict schoolmarm. "You're going to have to leave now. Pearl needs to rest."

Pearl grabbed Hannah's arm and pleaded silently with a slight shake of her head and reached for Hubert's hand.

Hannah gave them both a stern look but acquiesced. "All right." She turned to Hubert. "But it's up to you to see to it that she doesn't exert. The doctor wants her to stay quiet."

Hubert patted Pearl's hand. "I promise." To underscore his vow, he reached for the music box, turned the key, and lifted the lid. The sweet notes brought a smile to her heart as well as her lips. As soon as Hannah left, she reached for the paper and pencil again.

*Please don't go.*

Seeing the smile that creased Hubert's face and crinkled his eyes was worth risking Hannah's ire.

## sixteen

Pearl smiled as the doctor's wife repeated her admonishment not to speak more than necessary. Hannah was worse than a mother hen. Doc had given his permission that morning for Pearl to sit out on the sunny back porch of the doctor's residence. Hubert sat beside her on the porch swing.

Hannah draped a shawl around Pearl and warned her not to get chilled, then bustled back into the house. Hubert caught Pearl's eye, and they shared a chuckle. Since it was August, a chill was unlikely, but Hannah meant well.

"I'm so glad you're feeling better, my dear." Hubert's voice was still slightly raspy.

"It feels good to be outside." Her croaky whisper resembled that of a frog with the croup. "Who is running the store while you're here?"

Hubert raised a cautionary pointer finger and waggled it at her. "I love hearing your voice, but you'd best follow the doctor's orders."

Mercy sakes, she'd be glad when she could be up and about, doing the things she loved, instead of sitting here like a useless, voiceless sluggard. Impatience nipped at her, but then she remembered once again God's goodness in getting her out of the fire alive. Still in awe over Hubert's revelation of Everett's role in rescuing both of them, she sent another silent prayer to the throne room of heaven, asking God to heal Everett.

Hubert stood and crossed the porch where Hannah had left a tray with a pitcher of water and cups. He poured a cupful of water and brought it to Pearl, then reclaimed his seat beside her. "To answer your question, I hired young Phillip O'Dell to come work in the store part-time." Hubert grinned. "I'm not sure how many O'Dells there are. Phillip is a few years younger than Tillie, but he's her oldest brother. He's a bright youngster and a hard worker, and having him there frees me up to come and be with you and Everett."

The warm sun on her shoulders offered a cheery welcome to her first venture outdoors, and she drew in a cautious breath as deeply as she could. The fresh essence of the morning air was tainted by the stale scent of smoke that still lingered, a sinister reminder of the flames that nearly took Hubert's life and her own. And Everett's.

At some point, she knew she'd have to view the destruction and see what she could salvage. Her heart wept for the residents who had called the boardinghouse home for several years. Sheriff Webster hadn't elaborated on the degree of loss for her or her boarders. He'd only stated he thought the fire may have been purposely set. The very thought sent a sickening shiver through her.

Hubert tugged the shawl a little higher around her neck. "Are you cold?"

She shook her head. "Just thinking of the fire," she whispered.

He slipped an arm around her and patted her shoulder, as though reading her thoughts. "If you will allow me, I'd like to help you sift through the rubble when you feel up to it. No need to think of that today, though."

"What will my boarders do now?"

Hubert patted her hand. "Praise God none of them were there when the fire started. Mr. Hogan was on one of his sales trips. He said there is a rooming house in Clermont where he can stay. Miss Frick was at her dressmaker shop. Since she and Mrs. Pettigrew are such good friends, she has moved in with her. Mr. Gallimore was at the newspaper office, of course. Apparently there is a small room in the back of the office, and he plans to stay there for now. Mrs. Russell's nephew came yesterday and has taken her home to live with his family. When the school opens again next month, Miss Pendergrass will have to find a place to stay when she comes back. I heard the school board was looking into that."

Pearl nodded as Hubert addressed the situation of each of her former boarders, grieved that they lost whatever possessions they had, but grateful they were unharmed and had a place to stay.

Hubert shifted around, facing her more fully. "There is something else we need to talk about, or rather something I need to tell you."

She turned her eyes to him and saw his gaze leave her and slide downward, as if studying his boots suddenly became important.

"Hubert?"

He lifted his head back to face her, but the smile that forced the upturn of his lips didn't reach his eyes. The love she'd seen there for weeks was replaced by misgiving, and unease deepened the lines in his brow.

"Pearl, there are some things in my past that you need to know. I promised God I would be completely honest with you, but I wanted to wait until you were feeling better." He paused, his steady gaze holding hers. For a moment he inclined his head toward her like he was about to kiss her, but he halted and glanced right and left. Apparently rethinking his action, he leaned back against the swing's cushions.

"You already know that my first wife left me for another man, but you don't know why."

"Hubert—"

He held up his hand. "No, Pearl. Let me say this. The

doctor doesn't want you to talk, so please don't try. It's important that I confess everything to you."

Something akin to fear sent a slight jolt through her, but she nodded and folded her hands in her lap. Whatever was on his heart had carved obvious furrows of heartache through him, and she wasn't at all sure she wanted to hear it. She'd not yet told him she wished to renew their engagement. What if his disclosure changed the course of their relationship forever?

Hesitation edged his bearing. He pulled in an unsteady breath. "I went to work for the Pinkerton Detective Agency the same year Everett was born. From the start, I knew it was the career I wanted, and I was determined not to allow anything to interfere with my success." A scowl marred his features, and Pearl fought to stay her hand from smoothing out the crease between his eyes.

"Normally, the married men handled the investigations close to home and the single fellows were the ones who received the accolades for their daring exploits chasing down criminals." He shook his head. "I knew the more complicated cases would require me being away from home for long periods of time, but I began to push my superiors to assign those cases to me."

He closed his eyes and drew in his brows, his face a reflection of the painful memory. She wished she could tell him nothing from his past mattered. Her heart grieved to see his whole demeanor slumped as though he carried a heavy load.

"There were times I was away from home for two or three months at a time. I'd come home long enough to be congratulated for my good work, receive a citation or two in my personnel file, and I'd take another case even more difficult than the last."

He turned sorrow-filled eyes on her. "Pearl, I knew God

was speaking to my heart, telling me I should be home with my family, but I pushed everything aside—my family and my God—and allowed ambition to drive me. Prestige became my god." He rose from the swing and paced several steps away before turning and plodding back again. "Lucinda, my wife, began demanding that I resign from the Pinkertons. The more she demanded, the more determined I was to be the best agent in the country. About a week before Everett's eighth birthday, she told me she was planning a party and all Everett had requested was for his father to be there."

He turned and pressed his hands on the porch railing, his head hung like the demons of remembrance pushed his posture into submission. "The following day my superior received a wire about a notorious bank robber and murderer. Every time this man committed a crime, the story made the headlines. I knew if I was the one to bring him in, it would mean not only the esteem of my peers, but also the promotion in rank I sought." Derision laced his voice. "I talked my boss into letting me take the case, went home, and packed a bag. Lucinda railed at me and accused me of being married to my job. Everett cried and begged me to stay for his birthday party. I knew God was telling me to go back to the office and tell my boss I'd changed my mind. But I didn't. I left that afternoon."

Hubert's chin almost touched his chest. Pearl longed to reach out and take his hand and tell him not to say any more, but she couldn't. She sat suspended in time. How could the man she loved and respected be the same one he was describing?

"It took me almost four months, but I captured the man I was after. I turned my prisoner over to the U.S. marshal and stopped at the nearest telegraph office to send a wire to Lucinda, telling her I was coming home. I had no way of knowing it couldn't be delivered."

Pearl watched the raw memory batter the man she loved.

He cleared his throat repeatedly and continued. "I stopped on the way home and bought Everett an Orvis fishing rod and a brass reel with silk line. Thought he'd forgive me for missing his birthday if I brought him the best fishing rod money could buy." Hubert's voice cracked and he started coughing, whether from speaking too much or from emotion, Pearl couldn't tell.

He poured a bit of water into a cup and took several sips. His coughing subsided, but he remained several steps away from the swing, as though purposely holding himself apart from her. Didn't he know she longed to wrap her arms around his neck and whisper to him that he didn't need to say any more?

"When I discovered Lucinda and Everett were gone, I went directly to her parents. Everett was there, but I was told he didn't want to see me—that he hated me." He heaved a sigh. "They wouldn't tell me where Lucinda was. Her mother said I didn't deserve her daughter, that I didn't know how to be a good husband or father. A few days later I learned Lucinda left Baltimore with another man."

Weariness etched its signature all over Hubert. He turned slowly to face Pearl and raised his eyes to meet hers. "I hurt my family by letting success and my thirst for importance direct me, and I hurt myself by disobeying God. I've lived with the regret for more than twenty years." He held his hands out, away from his sides, palms up. "You had to know, Pearl. I couldn't ask you to spend the rest of your life with me, not knowing the truth. Now that you are aware of the kind of man I was, if you wish to terminate our relationship, I'll understand, and I won't persist in pressing you to change your mind."

He dropped his hands to his sides and moved toward her, his hesitant step uncharacteristic of his usual confidence.

"You need to rest now, Pearl. But there is just one question I must ask you." A flush filled his cheeks behind his beard. "Did Silas Cain really ask you to marry him?"

She glanced down at her folded hands on her lap and gave a small nod. "Yes."

Several moments of silence hung between them and Pearl lifted her eyes to light softly on the man standing before her. Dear Hubert—how she loved him.

She reached her hand out to him. "Come sit with me."

Hubert settled into the swing beside her and enclosed her hand between both of his. The warmth of his nearness gave her the courage to be as honest with him as he'd been with her.

"There is something I must tell you as well," she whispered. Hubert appeared about to protest, but she shook her head. "I must."

She took a few sips of water. "I don't know how much you've heard about Silas. He first came to Willow Creek seven years ago. He stayed at the boardinghouse, and it wasn't long before he began asking if he could court me. I told him I had no desire to be courted, but that didn't seem to stop him." She took another sip of water.

"After a few weeks, everyone in town knew Silas wanted to court me. It didn't seem to matter that I'd said no. Then one evening, Silas asked if he could speak to me out on the porch. He made a big show of getting down on his knee and asking me to marry him."

She began coughing, and Hubert nudged the cup of water. "Please, my dear, you don't need to say any more."

Pearl shook her head again. "Yes, I do." She sipped more water and set the cup aside. "The following day, everyone in town was congratulating me on my engagement. I tried to tell them there was no engagement because I'd refused Silas's proposal." She dipped her head. "Imagine my shock when a woman knocked on my door a few days later and told me she was looking for her husband, Silas Cain. My other boarders weren't home yet, but Silas was always the first one home in the afternoon, so I asked the woman to wait. When Silas came in, there was a confrontation. Silas and his wife went for a walk, but he came back without her."

She paused to cool her throat with more water. Hubert seemed to understand her need to tell him about the past chapter of her life, and he didn't insist she stop. After a minute, she went on, her voice not much more than a croaky whisper.

"Silas left very early the next morning. I don't know where his wife was; I didn't see her again. I assumed she went with him." She bowed her head. "Hubert, I felt so dirty. That poor woman! I know none of the blame was mine, but what if the news of Silas having a wife had gotten out? I could only imagine what that would do to my reputation. Why, it would make me look like a Jezebel. I kept the story to myself and prayed no one would ever find out. I've never told this to anyone until now."

Hubert squeezed her hand. "That's enough talking now. The sheriff has already told me what you wrote out concerning Cain's intentions and how he threatened you." He slid his arm around her shoulders. "It's behind you now. God has a future for us to look forward to."

&

Hubert sat forward in his chair beside Everett's bed, grateful for the doctor's permission to sit with his son. But he hadn't been prepared for the swathe of bandages or the swelling of Everett's face. Part of the burned area on one arm was exposed, and the sight of the angry, red flesh made Hubert's gut twist. He could only imagine what lay beneath the bandages.

"He's so still. I can barely see him breathing." Hubert sent a worried glance to the doctor on the other side of the bed.

Doc Vogel stuck the ends of his stethoscope into his ears and pressed the apparatus to Everett's chest. "He's breathing just fine."

"There's a rather pungent odor in here."

The doctor nodded and hung his stethoscope around his neck. "Part of the smell is the carbolic acid salve we're using on the burns. We're making a liniment with linseed oil and limewater to blot on the less serious burned area. But there is also some dead flesh that we're still cleaning off."

An involuntary shudder shook Hubert. "There's no more risk of infection?"

"I didn't say that." Doc gingerly pulled back part of the bandage on Everett's neck and the lower part of his face. "We're keeping the wounds clean and removing bits of burned skin and flesh as we are able. Until new skin grows to cover the burned areas, the risk of infection will exist, but he's showing some encouraging signs of healing."

Hubert peered at the grisly red, purple, and blackened wounds along Everett's jawline. An ache of commiseration surged through him, and he clenched his teeth to hold back a groan of sympathy.

Doc replaced the bandages and straightened. "I'm afraid he's going to have some rather ugly scars."

Hubert fixed his gaze on the part of Everett's face not covered by the clean, white bindings. The thought of the once-handsome features being disfigured by lasting effects of the fire spurred grief, and condemnation strangled him. If only Everett hadn't followed him into the burning house. Had circumstances taken a different turn, however, he and Pearl would both rest in the town cemetery now. He longed to hold Everett's hand but was fearful that any touch could bring pain. He wished he could take some of that pain and bear it for his son.

Everett stirred.

Hubert leaned forward and gently touched a finger to Everett's unscathed left hand. "I'm here, son."

A faint groan sounded from Everett's lips, and he moved his head slightly, a wince defining his forehead.

Doc Vogel glanced at his watch. "He's not due for another dose of laudanum for two hours. We'll wait to clean off any more dead skin and tissue until we can give him more pain medication."

"Father?"

Unspeakable joy filled Hubert at the sound of Everett's voice, however weak. "Yes son, I'm here."

"The quieter he stays the less pain he'll have," Doc Vogel advised. "I'll let you have a little time together, then he needs to rest."

Everett blinked. "Father, you're all right. Doctor Vogel told me you were, but I had to see for myself."

"Yes, I'm fine, son. Pearl is going to be all right as well, thanks to you. We both owe you our lives."

A slight shake of Everett's head accompanied the tiny dip of his eyebrows. "It wasn't me."

Hubert frowned, thinking surely he'd heard Everett's words incorrectly. Of course it had been Everett who'd dragged him and Pearl from the inferno. Sheriff Webster said so. Perhaps Everett was delusional from the medication.

"You don't have to talk, son. Just lie quiet." Hubert hoped his voice communicated soothing reassurance.

But Everett seemed insistent. "You don't understand, Father. It wasn't me. The smoke was so thick I was completely blinded. The fire was all around—all sides. Windows were breaking—"

"Shh, it's all right, son. Just be quiet now." But the more Hubert coaxed him to be quiet, the more determined Everett grew.

His fingers caught Hubert's and curled around them, as though driven by an urgency to make Hubert understand. "I knew I couldn't find you by myself. I needed help. I cried out to God—begged Him to help me find you."

Hubert froze. Could it be? Had God answered his petition he'd prayed more times than he could count? Tears slipped down Hubert's cheeks and a shout of praise began to gather within his chest, rising into his throat.

"I was lost in that smoke. . .had no hope of finding you or Mrs. Dunnigan. The walls were caving in. . .roof was next. No way out. God was the only one who could find you. I pleaded with Him to keep you safe and lead me to you. God found you, Father, not me." Serenity erased the anguish in Everett's eyes as he relaxed against the pillow. "And I found God."

# seventeen

Hubert stood outside the post office and broke the seal on the envelope from Zack Peterson, his old friend from the Pinkerton Agency. It had taken longer than he'd anticipated to hear back from Zack. Since Silas Cain had already left town, whatever information Zack was able to find on Cain would be of little use to Hubert now. But curiosity drove him to open the letter to see if any of his suspicions were confirmed.

He quickly scanned the pages, taking in the list of charges and arrest warrants. Cain was wanted in four different states on eleven warrants, and had left behind a trail of jilted women he'd defrauded of money and property. A few he'd married without mentioning he already had a wife. . .or two. Hubert snorted with disgust.

The last page described Cain's associations with known criminals and the seedy underworld of corruption, and included a list of several aliases Cain used. "Fletcher Cain, Silas Fletcher, Silas Riley, Terrance Smith."

Anger surged through Hubert. Pearl was just another woman on Cain's list. Hubert clenched his teeth and stifled a growl. How he wished he could slap the handcuffs on Cain himself.

He strode across the street to the mercantile to check with young Phillip O'Dell, his part-time clerk. Satisfied that Phillip had everything under control, Hubert headed down the boardwalk toward the sheriff's office. On the way, he stopped by the stage depot to speak with Sam, the ticket agent.

Sam's drooping suspenders hung off his shoulders as he peered out from the depot window and nodded his head with such vigor, his spectacles slid down his nose. "Yeah, Sheriff was already here askin' the same questions. I'll tell you the same thing as I told him." He pushed his lopsided spectacles back into place with two fingers. "That Cain fella was standin' here waitin' for me to open up the mornin' Miss Pearl's place burned." Sam stroked his chin. "First, he said he wanted to buy a ticket to Cedar Rapids. Then he asked how many stopovers there was between here and there." The agent pursed his lips and pulled his pencil from behind his ear. "Thought it kinda strange, but it weren't none of my business."

Hubert fixed his eyes on the agent. "What was strange?"

Sam shrugged. "When I told him the southbound stage wasn't due in until late afternoon, he changed his mind 'bout where he was headed. Asked what stage was due in first. I says the westbound. But as soon as I told him that stage stopped at Fort Dodge, he asked what was the last stop *before* Fort Dodge. I told him Otter Springs and don'tcha know, he bought a ticket to Otter Springs." The man shook his head like the information he'd just given made no sense.

"What's in Otter Springs?"

"That's just it. There ain't nothin' in Otter Springs 'cept a way station."

Why would Cain buy a ticket to the middle of nowhere? "Is there a telegraph in Otter Springs?"

Sam leaned his elbow on the edge of the counter and sniffed. "Sometimes. Lines are down more than they're workin'. But as I recall, I got a wire from there about a month ago. Maybe the lines are still up."

Hubert rolled the information over in his mind. "Can Cain buy another ticket in Otter Springs, maybe heading in another direction?"

"Sure. He could pick up the southbound to Des Moines. 'Course there's a few places in between where he could board a train, too."

"Thanks, Sam." Hubert continued on to the sheriff's office, armed with the letter from Zack Peterson.

Sheriff Webster was pouring himself a cup of coffee when Hubert entered the office. "Mornin', Mr. Behr."

"Good morning, sir." Hubert pulled Zack's letter from his pocket and held it out to the lawman. "I thought perhaps you'd be interested in this."

Webster arched his eyebrows and took the letter. He scanned it quickly and grunted. "Accordin' to what Miss Pearl's already told me, looks like he was plannin' on makin' her one of his victims."

Hubert set his jaw and nodded. "Based on the information in that letter and Pearl's statement, seems like you have enough for a conviction once Cain is apprehended."

"Don't make much sense, him settin' the fire, but I reckon it ain't the first time revenge was the motive for a crime." The sheriff scowled at the papers and wanted posters cluttering his desk. "I don't have anything on Cain here. I already checked. But I'll go through this pile again and look for those other names he used."

"I stopped by the depot this morning and talked to Sam."

Webster nodded. "I sent a wire to Otter Springs. I'll let you know if I find out anything and you can wire your Pinkerton friend. I notified the federal marshal at Fort Dodge, too. Maybe we'll get lucky."

The men shook hands and parted company. Hubert's desire to return to the doctor's place and speak with Pearl widened his anxious strides. He'd spent most of the night in prayer, partly for Everett's recovery and partly for Pearl. He'd waited as long as he could bear. If he didn't ask her today, his heart would burst.

இ

Tears gathered in the corners of Pearl's eyes as she listened to Tessa and Hannah outline their plans. The three women sat together in the morning sun on the back porch of the doctor's residence.

"I must have the sweetest friends on the face of the earth." Pearl's raspy voice and sore throat improved daily. She leaned forward to wrap one arm around Tessa and the other around Hannah. "Mercy sakes, I don't know what to say."

"You don't have to say anything." Tessa laughed. "Just let us show you how much you're loved."

Hannah patted Pearl's back and offered her the hanky she pulled from her apron pocket. While Pearl blotted her eyes, Hannah scooted her chair closer. "Two of the women in the ladies sewing circle have sewing machines now. Johannah Fredricksen's husband gave her one last Christmas." The doctor's wife rattled off her efficiently coordinated plans. "Ivy Swenson and Johannah will bring their machines. Hilda Stone, Florence Hoffner, and Vera Owens are going to do the cutting, and there will be four or five other women there as well, in addition to Tessa and me."

Tessa reached over and squeezed Pearl's hand. "Please let us do this for you."

"Do what?"

All three women turned. Hubert climbed the back porch steps.

"Oh, Hubert, these ladies want to have a sewing bee for me tomorrow at the church. They're going to—"

"All Pearl's clothes got burned up in the fire."

"We're going to sew some dresses, skirts, nighties, and under—" Tessa clapped her hand over her mouth and her cheeks glowed bright pink.

Hannah flapped her hands. "She needs everything, so the ladies are going to make a day of it and sew her a new wardrobe."

Pearl blinked back tears as she watched the reaction on Hubert's face. The smile that creased his face pulled his mustache into a crescent.

"That's a fine idea, ladies, and so gracious of you." Hubert crossed the porch and pulled one of the wicker chairs over next to Pearl's rocker. "I'd be happy to supply the yard goods."

Pearl started to protest, but he turned his soft gray eyes on her. The twinkle she saw there was more than she could resist.

"Please?" He wiggled his eyebrows.

She ducked her head so he wouldn't see her blush. "I don't know what I'm going to do with you!" Her attempt to sound exasperated failed miserably. Hubert's grin tingled her toes.

The wicker chair squeaked as Hubert lowered himself into it. "I spoke with Doc a few minutes ago, and he tells me you're doing fine. So why don't you and Tessa come over to the mercantile and pick out whatever you want."

*Doing fine.* Reality gnawed at her. She had no place to go, and she couldn't stay with the Vogels forever. If the doctor felt she was well enough to walk to the mercantile, she was well enough to find some place to stay. She couldn't impose on Tessa and her little family. They had no extra room. She supposed the hotel was her only option, albeit an expensive one. Her savings was small and wouldn't pay for a hotel room for very long without a means of income.

"Pearl?"

She snapped her attention back to the conversation. "You all are so generous. How is a body to say thank you?"

Hubert picked up her hand and drew it to his lips, placing a chaste kiss on her fingers. "Then I'll be expecting you and Tessa this afternoon."

Pearl's heart fluttered, and she tucked the moment away in her memory to enjoy later.

Hubert cleared his throat. "I have something else I'd like

to discuss with you, but I must beg the indulgence of these lovely ladies." He sent Tessa and Hannah an apologetic look. In unison, the pair rose and excused themselves, knowing smiles on both their faces.

As soon as they were alone on the porch, Hubert's expression turned serious. "I've done plenty of talking in the past few days, telling you those things I felt God prompting me to share with you." He ran his thumb up and down the underside of her fingers and fidgeted in his chair, causing a symphony of squeaks from the wicker.

She lifted her free hand and touched one side of Hubert's peppery beard. She knew this man as well as anyone could know another person, and everything about him stirred her. She held her breath as she waited for him to say what was on his mind. Surely he must be able to hear her pounding heart.

"The past several weeks have been sorely painful for me. When you broke our engagement, I didn't understand. I was so sure that you loved me." A wince flickered over his features. "I now know that Everett had something to do with your decision, and that he has since asked your forgiveness."

Pearl lowered her eyes for a moment. The events of the past week had changed everything, including the way she viewed Hubert's and Everett's relationship. Did it even matter why she broke the engagement? Yes, Hubert had been completely honest with her. It was time for her to reciprocate. She owed him that much.

"Hubert, first of all, I want to say that my reasons for ending the engagement have changed. But I still think I should explain."

He gave a slight nod but didn't interrupt.

"When Everett came to see me at the boardinghouse several weeks ago, he told me that reconciliation between the two of you would be impossible if we married. I couldn't do that to you. I couldn't come between you and Everett knowing how important your son is to you." Her throat tightened, and she swallowed several times trying to keep the tears at bay. "But the morning of the fire he came and apologized and told me he was wrong. He wanted your happiness and he said if marrying me made you happy, then he'd give his blessing."

Hubert's fingers squeezed hers, and she couldn't stop a tear from meandering down her cheek. Hubert gently wiped it away.

He pulled in a slow, measured breath. "When I was searching for you through the smoke, I was afraid I'd lost you forever. All I wanted was one more opportunity to tell you that I love you, and I don't want to live a single day without you. I never want us to be separated again this side of heaven." Still holding her hand, he slipped from the chair to one knee in front of her. "Will you, once more, agree to be my bride?"

Unchecked tears filled her eyes and overflowed. Oh, how she loved this man.

❧

Pearl clung to Hubert's hand as they sat at Everett's bedside telling him of their renewed plans to marry. The sight of the young man's bandages made her cringe, especially since he'd suffered the burns rescuing her and Hubert. There were no words to thank him for what he'd done.

"And so, son. . ." Hubert paused to glance at her, and the look he gave her made her catch her breath. He returned his gaze to Everett. "We've decided to postpone the wedding until you are able to be there with us. It's what we both want."

A shadow of a smile touched Everett's face, and he lifted his left hand toward his father who clasped it. "I'm pleased. . .that you're going to be happy." He looked at Pearl with genuine contrition in his eyes. "I hope you can forgive me."

She caught a glimpse of Hubert in Everett's features. He was part of the man she loved. "Of course, Everett. I'm praying for your recovery."

He frowned a bit, and she thought perhaps he was in pain. "The boardinghouse?"

Hubert shook his head. "It's a total loss. Pearl and I talked a little while ago. Since I moved into my house last year, the living quarters above the mercantile are empty. Pearl is going to stay there for a few weeks until the wedding."

Everett nodded his affirmation and a blush warmed Pearl's face. She dipped her head. . . .*until the wedding.* Her pulse picked up speed, and she silently chided herself. *Mercy sakes, folks are going to think we're behaving like a couple of moonstruck youngsters.*

"Hubert, I think we should let Everett rest now." They rose and told Everett they'd return to visit with him later.

Once they stepped back out onto the back porch, Hubert tucked Pearl's arm in his and tugged her toward the steps. "Let's go for a walk."

She hesitated. "Shouldn't we ask Doc first?"

"Why? He's not invited." Hubert's mustache twitched with amusement.

She flapped her hand at him and made a clucking sound with her tongue. "Hubert! You're incorrigible."

The smile that stretched across his face made the years fall away. He caught her hand as they strolled through the doctor's backyard, past the edge of town, across an expanse of meadow, toward a grove of willow trees that lined the meandering creek.

"Let's sit for a while." Hubert steered her to the creek bank. "I don't want you to get tired out."

A sweet memory tickled Pearl's mind. "Should I have brought a picnic? The last time we came to this place, we had a picnic." But it wasn't the picnic that made the recollection so sweet.

With his hand supporting her elbow, Hubert helped her

sit on a thick bed of grass. He bent to pluck some of the daisies and cornflowers scattered along the creek's edge, adding a few sprigs of purple clover. He handed her the flowers and sat beside her, reaching out to touch the side of her face. She sighed and pressed her cheek into the warmth of his hand.

"My Pearl." His tender eyes searched her face. "God is so good to give me another chance to be the kind of husband He wants me to be." His steady gaze fixed on her eyes and a tremble danced through her. "In a few weeks, as soon as Everett is better, we'll take our vows before our friends and neighbors at the church. But I wanted to give you and God a holy promise today, that I pledge my whole heart to our marriage. I offer my covenant to you that, with God's help, I'll seek His wisdom and leading for us, and I will love you with everything within me until my last breath."

With that pronouncement, he inclined his head toward hers and placed the gentlest of kisses on her lips.

# epilogue

"Nervous?"

Pearl glanced at her groom and caught the wink he sent her. "Mercy sakes, no. Why should I be nervous?"

Hubert chuckled. "Most brides are."

She couldn't seem to stop smiling, and her eyes locked onto his. "But we aren't like most brides and grooms, are we?"

Hubert appeared to contemplate her question. "I don't suppose we are. We have a few extra years and some strands of silver hair, but that doesn't change how much we love each other."

"Nor does it change the way God has blessed us."

Pastor Witherspoon would call for the wedding to start in a matter of minutes, but Pearl wanted to capture this moment and etch it into her memory where nothing and no one could steal it. Their friends milled around, lingering after the Sunday morning service to witness the nuptials. Happy anticipation of the celebration to follow buzzed through the congregation, but Pearl blocked out everything but Hubert.

She leaned close to his ear. "I'm so grateful God gave us another chance."

Hubert's smile stole her breath. "I'm grateful you said yes."

"All right now, folks." Pastor Witherspoon beckoned to the congregation. "Let's take our places. Hubert, you and Pearl stand right here."

Pearl smoothed the bodice of the soft blue brocade dress the ladies had helped her sew for her wedding. Tessa handed her a bouquet of black-eyed Susans and purple coneflowers and stepped over to stand on Pearl's left side. Everett, bandages still binding one hand and arm and swathing one side of his face and neck, stood to the right of Hubert.

The pastor cleared his throat. "We almost didn't get to see this wedding happen. If it hadn't been for Everett here and the way God used him, Hubert and Pearl might not have been here for this day. So we first want to lift our praise and thanks to God for allowing this union to take place."

Hubert squeezed her hand, and she caught a glimpse of Everett from the corner of her eye. He was smiling.

Pastor Witherspoon continued. "So friends, we are gathered here in the presence of God and this company to witness the joining of this man and this woman in holy matrimony."

The words of the traditional vows as the pastor spoke them and Hubert echoed fell sweetly on Pearl's heart. When it came time for her to repeat her promise to love, honor, cherish, and obey, the precious vows spilled from her lips without any prompting.

Hubert took her left hand and slid a gold band onto her fourth finger. The pastor was speaking, but Pearl's senses were fixed on the gift God had given her, the man standing before her, holding her hand. Their love, forged and strengthened by God, had been tried, refined, and revealed by fire and had emerged as pure gold.

"You may kiss your bride now, Hubert." The pastor's words broke through her consciousness.

Her groom cupped her face gently in his hands. Pearl's eyes closed, a prayer of gratitude forming in her heart as a benediction on their first kiss as husband and wife.

# A Letter To Our Readers

Dear Reader:

In order that we might better contribute to your reading enjoyment, we would appreciate your taking a few minutes to respond to the following questions. We welcome your comments and read each form and letter we receive. When completed, please return to the following:

Fiction Editor
Heartsong Presents
PO Box 719
Uhrichsville, Ohio 44683

1. Did you enjoy reading *Revealing Fire* by Connie Stevens?
   ❏ Very much! I would like to see more books by this author!
   ❏ Moderately. I would have enjoyed it more if

   _____

   _____

   _____

2. Are you a member of **Heartsong Presents**? ❏ Yes ❏ No
   If no, where did you purchase this book? _____

   _____

3. How would you rate, on a scale from 1 (poor) to 5 (superior), the cover design? _____

4. On a scale from 1 (poor) to 10 (superior), please rate the following elements.

   | | | |
   |---|---|---|
   | ____ Heroine | | ____ Plot |
   | ____ Hero | | ____ Inspirational theme |
   | ____ Setting | | ____ Secondary characters |

5. These characters were special because? _____

_____

_____

6. How has this book inspired your life? _____

_____

_____

7. What settings would you like to see covered in future
   **Heartsong Presents** books? _____

_____

_____

8. What are some inspirational themes you would like to see
   treated in future books? _____

_____

_____

9. Would you be interested in reading other **Heartsong
   Presents** titles? ❏ Yes ❏ No

10. Please check your age range:
    ❏ Under 18              ❏ 18-24
    ❏ 25-34                 ❏ 35-45
    ❏ 46-55                 ❏ Over 55

Name_____

Occupation _____

Address_____

City, State, Zip_____

E-mail _____

# ALOHA BRIDES

## 3 stories in 1

$G$iven the opportunity to experience true love in the lush Hawaiian Islands, will three historical couples welcome it or allow fear to drive it away?

Contemporary, paperback, 368 pages, 5.1875" x 8"

# Presents

## Great Inspirational Romance
## at a Great Price!

**Heartsong Presents** books are inspirational romances in contemporary and historical settings, designed to give you an enjoyable, spirit-lifting reading experience. You can choose wonderfully written titles from some of today's best authors like Wanda E. Brunstetter, Mary Connealy, Susan Page Davis, Cathy Marie Hake, Joyce Livingston, and many others.

*When ordering quantities less than six, above titles are $3.99 each.*
*Not all titles may be available at time of order.*

---

HEARTSONG
PRESENTS

# If you love Christian romance...

$12.⁹⁹

You'll love Heartsong Presents' inspiring and faith-filled romances by today's very best Christian authors...Wanda E. Brunstetter, Mary Connealy, Susan Page Davis, Cathy Marie Hake, and Joyce Livingston, to mention a few!

When you join Heartsong Presents, you'll enjoy four brand-new, mass-market, 176-page books—two contemporary and two historical—that will build you up in your faith when you discover God's role in every relationship you read about!

Mass Market 176 Pages

Imagine...four new romances every four weeks—with men and women like you who long to meet the one God has chosen as the love of their lives...all for the low price of $12.99 postpaid.

To join, simply visit www.heartsong presents.com or complete the coupon below and mail it to the address provided.

✂ - - - - - - - - - - - - - - - - - - - - - - - -

# YES! Sign me up for Heart♥ng!

**NEW MEMBERSHIPS WILL BE SHIPPED IMMEDIATELY!**
**Send no money now.** We'll bill you only $12.99 postpaid with your first shipment of four books. Or for faster action, call 1-740-922-7280.

NAME_____

ADDRESS_____

CITY_____ STATE _____ ZIP _____

**MAIL TO: HEARTSONG PRESENTS, P.O. Box 721, Uhrichsville, Ohio 44683**
**or sign up at WWW.HEARTSONGPRESENTS.COM**